How come none of the ever-punctual teachers were at Cinder Creek School, when the kids arrived one morning? And why were all the usually-locked doors *unlocked* in the old school house set in the remote California valley?

And when Johnny and Ken set out to walk to the nearest house with a phone, why was it that someone didn't want them to cross the old bridge—their only means of escape. Someone who fired a rifle to stop them. The radio didn't work, the telephone wires were cut: the thirteen kids might have been the only people alive on earth.

And then the old yellow school bus came hurtling down the road "as if a maniac were at the wheel".

THE DAY
THE WORLD
WENT AWAY

OTHER DOUBLEDAY SIGNAL BOOKS

Austrian, Geoffrey
THE TRUTH ABOUT DRUGS

Biemiller, Ruth
DANCE: THE STORY OF KATHERINE DUNHAM

Brownmiller, Susan
SHIRLEY CHISHOLM: A BIOGRAPHY

Clarke, John
BLACK SOLDIER

Moore, Chuck
I WAS A BLACK PANTHER

Preston, Edward
MARTIN LUTHER KING: FIGHTER FOR FREEDOM

Terzian, James and Cramer, Kathryn
MIGHTY HARD ROAD: THE STORY OF CESAR CHAVEZ

Anne Elaine Schraff

THE DAY
THE WORLD
WENT AWAY

Doubleday & Company, Inc.
Garden City, New York

ISBN: 0-385-08068-9 Trade
0-385-00455-9 Paper
Library of Congress Catalog Card Number 72–92239
Copyright © 1973 by Doubleday & Company, Inc.
All Rights Reserved
Printed in the United States of America

Prepared by Rutledge Books
First Edition

1826639

CONTENTS

1. Where Are the Teachers?   1
2. Trouble at the Bridge   11
3. The Yellow Bus   19
4. The Fire   35
5. The Breakout   46
6. Dany Disappears   60
7. The Strangers   68
8. Hide or Surrender?   80
9. The Death of Janet?   95
10. The Three Escape   107
11. "Better Than Dying"   117
12. "But We Had Some Good Ideas"   126

1. Where Are the Teachers?

On the morning of March twenty-third, thirteen teen-agers boarded the big yellow bus at various locations across the spacious mauve valley for the ride to Cinder Creek Rural High School.

"But where are the teachers' cars?" Danielle Frazer asked as the bus came to a smooth halt at its usual stopping point. She was a small girl with a tense, pinched face.

There were four teachers, including the principal, at Cinder Creek. Mr. Farnsworth, the principal, who also taught math and science, usually drove Mr. Watt, the phys. ed. teacher. Mrs. Boswell and Miss Onslow always came together. So actually only two cars were missing from the dirt parking area. But it did look oddly empty.

"Teachers are tardy!" Charlie Gilman laughed. "Let's give 'em all detention slips when they come."

The thirteen filed off the bus, most of them saying something to Mr. Ainsley, the bus driver, like "see you" or "smooth ride today" or just simply "by now." Mr. Ainsley answered, "Have a good day. See you all this afternoon, good Lord willing and the creeks don't rise." He was a skinny, amiable old man who said the same thing every morning, rain or shine—but then, this morning, he added philosophically, "Long as the old world's spinning, guess I'll be making my rounds."

"That was odd," tawny-haired Valerie Roman said when she was outside the bus. "I don't remember him ever saying anything like that before."

Margaret Illiam, a seventeen-year-old senior, adjusted her brown-rimmed, thick-lensed glasses on her small nose. "I imagine even Mr. Ainsley has been reading about the ecological crisis," she said, without smiling. "I mean, it must give everybody a complex to realize how close we are to total disaster."

"You mean the world is going to stop spinning?" Charlie laughed.

"Yeah," Red McGinnis chimed in, nodding his red head solemnly. "Like it's gotten too heavy to spin, y'see?"

"Really, boys!" Margaret said sternly, her small, serious face mature for her years. "Sometimes I think you have nothing between your ears but bone!"

"Do you remember Mr. Farnsworth ever being late?" Danielle Frazer asked Gayle Cherneck—they were both sophomores. Perspiration dampened the palms of Danielle's hands. She had once read that damp palms are sometimes a sign of a nervous illness, so she was afraid to tell her father about them.

Gayle was chubby and almost, but not quite, pretty. "No, he's always been on time. I thought he must get here with the first rooster's crow."

"Well, he's late today," Valerie said. She was the first to reach the school door. She didn't expect it to be open because if none of the teachers were here, who would have opened it? But, out of force of habit, she tried the door anyway and to her surprise it was open. "Look, somebody's unlocked it."

Charlie slapped his thigh in high spirits. "Wow, they're really goofing up! They're not only late this morning but last night they must have forgotten to lock up the old P.O.W. camp!"

"Yeah," Red agreed. "Trouble at Stalag Cinder Creek!"

The school building was red brick, built many years earlier, in the late 1920s. There had been a flourishing mining operation in the mountains behind Cinder Creek in those days, but the 1929 depression had shut it down. Back in the twenties almost seventy students attended the four-room school. Now there were just thirteen and next year there would be half that number,

3

and probably the district would at long last close the school.

One of the seniors who would graduate this year was Johnny Harrison, tall, part Cherokee, with skin the color of the red earth of the valley. He followed Valerie into the building. "Hey, anybody around?" he called. But there was no answer.

"It's kind of spooky, isn't it?" Valerie said slowly. Usually the school day began in Room 1, where everybody took United States or world history with a sprinkling of civics and current events. Mrs. Bernice Boswell, a portly middle-aged lady, taught those classes. Valerie tried the door to Room 1 and found it open, surprising herself again. Mr. Farnsworth had a strict rule that all rooms as well as the building itself be locked each evening. In recent years, as the valley population declined, transients drifted through, staying overnight in empty and unlocked buildings and taking whatever wasn't nailed down.

"I can't see everybody slipping up like this last night," Johnny said softly.

The thirteen filed haphazardly into Room 1. Charlie gave Red a playful shove, and they wrestled in the back of the room until they eventually overturned a globe stand. Then Charlie squeezed his oversized body into a desk and sighed from the exertion of his horseplay with Red. The two boys were a lot alike, except in build. Red was bony and angular with unruly red hair and freckles tumbling over his face like blobs of ginger.

"You know," Charlie said, "my old man is really after me about grades. If I don't get them up this quarter, he's not going to let me buy that old car I want."

Red shrugged. "I don't get a car no matter what I do in my stupid schoolwork. My father hasn't worked in a coupla months." But, the boy thought with passing bitterness, his father found enough money for liquor. Not that he blamed him that much. All his luck had been bad and the worst had come when Red's mother died. She was the glue that held the home together, and after she was gone everything began to come slowly unstuck until now it was hardly a home any more.

"I'm not cut out for studying that dull history junk or silly old poetry," Charlie complained.

Gayle had been watching the boys. Now she said, "Some of the poems in our book are pretty good. I don't mind Frost."

"Yuk," Charlie sneered and Gayle's moon face turned tragic. She tried so hard to say the right things but she always missed out. Maybe, she thought, I sometimes try too hard.

"I ought to be in trade school or something, learning mechanical stuff," Charlie continued.

"Fat chance around here." Red doodled geometric

patterns on the top of his desk with a red ball-point pen. "In this nowheresville we're lucky we even got any kind of school." Red didn't know what he wanted to do with his life, but he did know he would do it far from here, far from this wilderness, far from the creaky old house where he and his father spent hours with nothing to say to each other.

Gayle turned to Danielle, who was her closest friend. They had nothing in common except loneliness, but that was enough. Gayle was too chubby to be popular, Danielle too shy. "Dany, I'm going to lose thirty pounds before summer."

"I think you'd be so pretty, Gayle, if you lost a few pounds," Danielle said in her soft, almost inaudible voice. "I mean, you've got the features to be beautiful." Her small eyes roamed across the room, pausing at each boy. None of them liked her, she realized dismally. It must be her personality, she told herself. If only she didn't get so frightened whenever she spoke to a boy that the words stuck in her throat like a fishbone!

Hugh Davis, a big-muscled eighteen-year-old senior, was pacing around the room restlessly, unwilling to take a seat as some of the others had done. His sister, Sandra, sixteen and a junior, was at her desk, her notebook out and ready. "Hey," Hugh snapped at her, "the lady isn't even here yet. What're you doing?"

Sandra brushed her short hair back from her

creamed-coffee skin. "I'm being prepared, Hugh. Nothing wrong with that."

"Sometimes I think you crawled into a textbook in first grade and you never came all the way out again," Hugh said, angry at the girl who was no brighter than he was, but who made much better grades.

Sandra smiled slightly. "Dad wouldn't mind if you did a little crawling into your textbook, Hugh."

The angry frown remained on the black senior's face. "You so sure that when you finish cracking those books they'll lay down the welcome mat for you in one of those big medical schools you got your little heart set on?"

Sandra stopped smiling. "Mr. Farnsworth said I could easily handle a premed course and I don't see any reason why I won't get into a good college."

Hugh laughed harshly. "Two reasons why—you're black and you're a girl. You been reading too many silly rose-colored stories about the great new world of equality and love."

"And you," Margaret Illiam broke in, "are a negative person, Hugh Davis. Sandra will be a fine doctor and I will be a splendid lawyer, and we'll have a nice *I told you so* worked in needlepoint especially for you."

Sandra laughed, and Hugh turned away.

"Hey, look!" Charlie pointed at the clock. "It's almost

nine and the jailers haven't arrived. You think we ought to make a break for it?"

Johnny glanced at Valerie. "I think I'll go to the office and call somebody, see what's up."

"I'm coming along." Hugh caught up to Johnny and both boys went down the short hallway to the principal's office. Johnny's hand closed over the doorknob. "Oh, great. It's locked."

The boys looked at each other, bewildered.

"Would you want to bust open the door?" Johnny suggested.

Hugh shook his head. "Be our luck to have Farnsworth drive up just then and stick us with the repair bill."

Johnny nodded. "Yeah. We better wait awhile longer, I guess."

When they returned to Room 1, Johnny announced matter-of-factly, "Office door is locked." But Valerie looked closely at his face and she detected a concern there that he had deliberately kept out of his voice.

"I'm not surprised old Farny locked his own office." Charlie chuckled. "I mean, what if some nasty burglar got all his girlie magazines?"

Red burst out laughing, but Bennie Bryce, a senior, said irritably, "Come off it, Charlie."

Charlie turned defensive. "You don't know everything, Bryce. I mean, so you can remember a lot of useless junk on tests and you play the piano—big deal!"

Johnny leaned against the wall near where Valerie sat, his eyes uneasily on the hands of the clock as they passed nine, then nine-fifteen, and edged toward nine-thirty. "Can't figure this," he said softly to her.

Her pale blue eyes shadowed like a clear lake when clouds move overhead. "I can't either. They wouldn't just not come without sending word."

Johnny nodded. When he came across a problem, he dealt with it. He was an impatient person, and it was hard for him to just stand around and wonder what was going on.

Across the room, Suzanne Pauley, a senior, talked to Janet Quantrain. "I wish I'd brought my guitar. I could have practiced the new song I wrote."

Janet stared at the older girl in admiration. "Oh, did you write a new one?"

Suzanne smiled, enjoying the adulation. "Yes. I just sort of knocked it out last night when my grandparents were asleep. I went out on the back porch and blocked it out on the guitar and scribbled the words. It was easy. When I hear that junk those creeps are singing on the radio, I just know that if I got the right breaks I could be on my way."

"Let me hear your song, Suzy," Janet asked eagerly.

"I can't, not without my guitar."

"Oh please, just a little bit of it."

Suzanne shrugged. "Actually it isn't the best I ever wrote. And I only remember the first verse." She began singing softly in a mediocre but throaty voice. "Dream upon a summer day . . . dream your loneliness away . . . dream awhile, and when you smile . . . dream another dream that's light and gay. . . ."

"Oh Suzy, it's so *true!*" Janet cried in appreciation.

But Suzanne noticed Charlie staring at her and her mood changed abruptly. "Are we just going to sit here all day like zombies? Isn't anyone going to *do* anything?"

"Yeah," Charlie agreed, "let's go home. The show is not going on as scheduled. Old Farney and his crew took a holiday."

"This *isn't* a holiday of some kind, is it?" Danielle asked.

"Yeah," Charlie answered unkindly, "it's the Fourth of July and we all forgot!"

Red took up the game. "Naw, it's Christmas. Deck the halls with boughs of ivy—or is it holly? Anyway, tralalalala. . . ."

"Oh shut up, you silly idiots," Margaret complained, wiping her glasses with a tissue. She turned to Valerie. "What *are* we going to do?"

A grim, resolute look came over Johnny Harrison's dark face. "We are going to get into the principal's office one way or another and find out just what is going on around here!"

2. Trouble at the Bridge

Bennie looked up with interest. "I picked a lock last year when my dad accidentally locked his keys inside the tool shed."

"Good," Johnny said. "Come on and we'll see what we can do." Hugh followed and the three boys walked swiftly to the principal's office.

Bennie knelt on the floor and fiddled quietly with various keys, then with a nail file and a small screw driver. Most of the others gathered along the hallway to watch. Finally Bennie sighed and gave up. "I'm afraid it's a deadlocking pin."

Hugh nodded. "Farnsworth bragged about having a foolproof lock on his office. Said it was important because all our records are in there. Well, Johnny, should we bust the door down?"

Johnny agreed without hesitation. Both boys were

over six feet and weighed around one seventy-five. But when they pitted their strength against the heavy old door, it would not yield.

"It's solid oak, well built," Bennie said. "In the old days they built things much stronger." Bennie was only five feet six inches himself, narrow shouldered and slim. "I'm very puzzled," he went on. "I mean, why should just this door be locked? And both Mr. Farnsworth's car and Miss Onslow's car not working? And even if such a coincidence did happen, wouldn't they find other means to get here?"

"I say let's split, right now," Charlie shouted from the hallway, the first sign of worry in his eyes. Before now it had been a delightful joke, a pleasant happening. Now he too wondered what was going on.

"How do we split?" Johnny asked reasonably. "The nearest any of us lives from here is five miles. For most of us it's ten miles."

"How about some of us walking to that old house near the bridge over Cinder Creek?" Margaret suggested. "About a mile down the road from here, isn't it?"

"Yeah," Johnny said. "Old couple lives there—the Halsteads. I'm sure they have a phone."

"Thank heaven we're finally getting somewhere," Suzanne said, and immediately went back to her daydreaming.

"I'll go," Hugh offered quickly, eager for the chance to do something.

"Hold on," Charlie cautioned. "I mean . . . look, maybe that old guy and his wife never even saw a black guy before and they'd be too scared to even open their door."

"Okay, why don't you go, Charlie?" Hugh said harshly.

"I would," Charlie said, flushing, "only I sprained my ankle the other day and I . . . ah . . . might not make it."

"Sure, sure," Hugh sneered.

"I'll go," Johnny offered, and immediately Suzanne looked at Ken and smiled. "Why don't you go with him, Kenny?"

Ken had been an all-around athlete back in Van Nuys, California, when his father had decided to quit the "rat race" of his Wilshire Boulevard brokerage for the great outdoors, where he could afford to be a gentleman farmer.

Ken warmed instantly under Suzanne's encouraging smile. "Sure, I'm with you, Johnny. We can both make good time."

"Let's go," Johnny said and got to his feet. The eleven who were to remain behind followed the two boys outside and waved them off. Then they gathered under the two cottonwood trees where they usually had lunch. A cool breeze was blowing but the bright sunshine prevailed.

"It's so quiet," Valerie said to Margaret, as the two girls sat down on a bench. Margaret smiled in appreciation of the silence. "Yes, it's beautiful, isn't it?"

Sandra Davis came over to join them. "Did you ever hear it so quiet?"

"I was saying the same thing just now to Maggie," Valerie answered.

"We're so accustomed to awful noise pollution," said Margaret, "that silence frightens us."

"Yes, I'm scared all right," Valerie admitted, clasping her arms around her slender body. "I mean, I don't know exactly why, but it's *too* quiet. . . ."

"I don't even hear the birds," Sandra said. "It's weird."

Charlie came strolling over, looking for diversion. "What's this? No birds singing? It could be prophetic what the old bus driver said this morning, remember? 'Long as the old world's spinning.' Maybe it stopped."

He looked at the girls to see what effect he'd had, enjoying the shock on the face of Danielle, who sat at a nearby table, close enough to hear.

She cried shrilly, "Stop that stupid talk. It's all crazy, stupid!" Fear came easily to Danielle and with dreadful intensity.

But Charlie did not understand and he continued the

teasing. "Like, there's thirteen of us, right? And right there is a bad omen."

"Oh, Charlie!" Margaret tossed her two thin brown braids. "You are a dum-dum. We have been thirteen since the semester began and nothing catastrophic has happened before."

"Unless you count having Charlie in our midst," Hugh put in.

But Charlie would not be stopped. "Way I see, it's been fate all the way. Remember that black cat that hung around the school in November?"

Danielle began to tremble and Gayle put her arm around the slighter girl's shoulders. "Oh, don't let him bug you, Dany."

"But it is awfully strange how we're all alone here and the teachers aren't coming." Danielle's voice was high pitched, and now it rose higher. "And we *are* thirteen, like he said. . . ."

"Hogwash!" Margaret said firmly. "Or poppycock, as my father says."

"In about half an hour," Valerie put in, forcing her voice to be cheerful, "Johnny and Ken will reach the Halstead place, telephone town and find out that something perfectly ordinary happened to delay school. Then probably Mr. Ainsley will bring the bus early to pick us up. And we'll all feel pretty foolish that we dreamed up a lot of silly ideas." But Valerie didn't really believe it would happen that way. She hoped that it would, but she didn't really believe it.

"Hear, hear!" Red laughed. "Let's hear it for the cheer-up girl of the month." Red really liked Valerie, liked her long, shiny blond hair, her usually merry blue eyes. He would have liked to date her, even asked her once, but she told him nicely but firmly that she had this thing going with Johnny.

Ken and Johnny took the only road leading from the school to the farm near the bridge. The school lay in a small valley sheltered by steep, rocky hills. The only entrance to the valley was across a wooden bridge that spanned Cinder Creek. The Halsteads lived about a fourth of a mile beyond the bridge crossing.

"Did you ever talk to that old couple, Johnny?"

"A few times in town. They're almost eighty now and sometimes Suzanne's grandparents drive them around for shopping."

"You're sure they have a phone?"

"Yeah."

Ken was pleased with the idea that he would participate in "rescuing" Suzanne and the others. He hoped he could ride in with Mr. Ainsley, perhaps get out and explain everything. It might impress Suzanne enough so that she'd give more attention to him. He'd been trying to date Suzanne—she was about the prettiest girl he'd ever seen anywhere, but she had that pretty face buried in those silly fan magazines most of the time, dreaming about becoming a big record star, getting on television and all that. Ken had tried to tell her how it was in Los Angeles, how kids were coming in droves trying to land recording contracts and how most of them ended up with broken hearts. But she just turned cold at that line of talk. Now maybe she would see him in a better light and this long hard walk would mean something.

The bridge was now within view, and the boys moved more quickly. Cinder Creek ran fast and deep in the winter and early spring, fed by the melting snows of the mountains, and Johnny had often wondered why the city fathers hadn't built a sturdier bridge across it, since the school would be isolated if ever anything happened to the frail wooden bridge.

Johnny reached the beginning of the bridge a few feet ahead of Ken. "I can see the Halstead windmill ——" he began, but then his voice was lost in the burst of loud gunfire that spattered the air. At first Johnny thought it was thunder from a sudden storm blowing up over the mountains, but then he saw bullets ripping into the bridge a few yards ahead of him, slashing and splintering the ancient wood.

"Somebody's up there in the rocks!" Ken screamed. Johnny turned and moved quickly back. Instantly there was silence from the sniper. The sun glinted off the sheer granite walls. The boys could have almost believed that nothing had happened had it not been for the acrid residue of smoke lingering in the air.

Ken's face was as pale as the alkali flats of the desert and his hands trembled. "Let's get out of here before they kill us!"

. "But the bridge!" Johnny cried. "It's our only way out of here—"

"They'll never let us across," Ken said hoarsely. "Come on, let's get out of rifle range!"

The boys turned and headed back into the valley. Fury burned in Johnny's eyes. "We'll wait until it gets dark and then we'll make it across."

"Johnny, listen." Ken spoke softly, his lips trembling. "Mr. Ainsley is due at the school at three o'clock. I mean, just because the teachers didn't come doesn't mean that he won't come either. Why he's never been late, Johnny, much less not come at all."

His voice trailed away as Johnny's sharp eyes met his. "Ken, do you really think Mr. Ainsley is going to drive up in that old yellow school bus and park in front of our little red schoolhouse like on any other day? Do you really think that?"

Ken looked at the other boy silently, then turned away, and they continued to walk back toward the school.

By now it was eleven-thirty.

3. The Yellow Bus

"They're coming back already," Valerie shouted, seeing the two figures heading toward the schoolyard.

Heads turned. All eyes were fastened on the returning boys. Not even Charlie could think of an appropriate joke, and Red's long jaw was set.

It was Bennie who spoke first, while the boys were still a hundred yards off. "They didn't make it. Look at their faces." A gasp of dismay followed that pronouncement as the others found the same message in the boys' grim expressions.

"What happened?" Hugh demanded.

"We got to the beginning of the bridge and somebody began shooting at us. There was no way to cross that bridge," Johnny said tautly.

"Shooting?" Gayle asked incredulously.

"But I don't understand." Danielle shoved back

her long hair with nervous jabs and tears started in the corners of her eyes. "Why would anybody do that?"

"Maybe that old man," Charlie suggested. "Maybe he's nuts or something and he just sits there shooting at people for kicks."

"I doubt it," Johnny said. "From what I've seen of him he's a nice old guy."

"Could be some crazy hunter I suppose," Hugh said hopefully. "Maybe he wasn't even shooting at you guys. Maybe he thought he saw a jackrabbit or something."

"No chance." Johnny shook his head emphatically. "They meant to keep us from crossing that bridge." Ken nodded in agreement.

"But why?" Danielle demanded, the tears spilling and making bright tracks on her pale cheeks.

"Oh Dany," Margaret said brusquely, "pull yourself together! The boys don't know why. If they knew they would tell us." Margaret disliked weakness in anybody but especially in girls. It gave substance to what she considered to be the myth of the weak, hysterical female doomed to a life of subservience to the stronger male.

Bennie frowned. "I just can't understand this at all. I mean, it's like the whole world's gone crazy. Hey, wait—there's a radio in Room 2. Let's turn it on and see if we get any clues."

"Good idea," Margaret said promptly. Of all the boys

20

at school, Margaret admired Bennie the most. He was cool and bright and Margaret valued both qualities.

The thirteen hurried into Room 2 quickly. Hugh was first to the radio and he flipped it on and waited. Usually it warmed up immediately but now it only produced a dead silence. He checked to see whether it was plugged in and, finding that it was, he crossed the room and tried the light switch. It clicked uselessly. "The electricity is out," he declared flatly.

Danielle covered her mouth with her hand, but the scream escaped through her fingers. Even Gayle began to sniffle. "Shut up, will you?" Margaret snapped. "Oh honestly, will acting like crybabies help anything at all?"

"Electricity has probably been out all along," Bennie said. "We just didn't notice because that classroom clock works on a battery. Does anybody have a transistor radio in his locker?"

"I would if the World Series was going on," Charlie said.

"There's a battery radio in Mr. Farnsworth's office," Margaret remembered. "He told me once that if the lights ever go out at least we'll be able to hear what's happening on the radio."

"But we can't get into his office," Suzanne reminded her. She stared discontentedly around Room 2—the horrible old-fashioned desks, the ancient chalkboard with hundreds of weeks of dust still trapped in the wooden trays. She hated these rooms, this school, the valley itself. She also hated living with her grandparents on that miserable ranch just because her father had to be working for the government somewhere in Asia and it was "too dangerous" for Suzanne out there.

"You know," Suzanne's voice was bitter, "it just figures that something like this should happen in this awful, disgusting place. I mean, less than three months to my graduation and I've been just living to get out of here and now this, like something out of a horror movie. Perhaps those awful hicks in town are doing this to us on purpose."

Janet Quantrain listened with great interest, nodding in agreement. Everything that Suzanne said carried much weight with her. "You know," Janet said, "Suzy may be right. I mean, my dad is always complaining that I don't appreciate all the advantages I've got. He says how lucky I am to be getting almost individual instruction in this wonderful school—how dedicated the teachers are, and all that. He can't understand why I don't get better grades. Maybe he and the others are playing sort of a joke on us."

Margaret rolled her eyes heavenward in disgust. "I can just imagine my father leaving his chem lab to play Halloween tricks on us."

"My dad might," Red said. Since his father had been drinking so much the ranch was going downhill fast. He had no spirit, but he did frequently express disappointment in Red for being lazy. "I bet my dad would like to scare the living daylights out of me."

"Don't be ridiculous," Johnny snapped. "They were shooting real bullets at us."

"But they didn't hit you," Charlie pointed out. Charlie's father sold farm equipment all around the valley. He had a million stories of his own tough childhood and how Charlie failed to be thankful for his relatively easy life. "My dad can really be mean sometimes. He locked me in the tool shed all night once when I was a little kid just to teach me not to sneak out at night. I was really scared, but he just laughed and said it served me right."

"I can just imagine Grandfather convincing the teachers not to come today," Suzanne continued. "I can see him convincing them to shut off the electricity and keep us here for a while to think over our evil ways!"

"I'll bet old Ainsley was in on it too," Charlie said eagerly. "That's how come he said that stuff about the world spinning this morning. He was setting the stage for the plot."

Danielle looked at Gayle. "Do you think it could be?"

Gayle shrugged. "I wouldn't put it past my folks. Mom is always nagging me about eating too much and not working hard enough at school." And spending all her time thinking about boys, but Gayle didn't want to repeat that.

Ken Tillich frowned. "I can't buy that." But he had no other explanation—not one he wanted to talk about or even think about, anyway.

It was twelve noon, and Charlie dug into his lunch pail for his usual three sandwiches. Red did the same, but most of the others had little appetite. Johnny and Valerie walked a bit away from the others and paused in the shade of a large cottonwood. Valerie looked up at the Indian boy she had known since early childhood, wondering. Their parents had adjacent ranches and it was Johnny who had taught her how to ride, coaxing her when she tumbled off the gentle paint gelding, applauding when she learned to handle the horse. It was Johnny who had shown her secret places in the wilderness like the warm water pools where the pupfish miraculously survived. He had a great reverence for life in all its forms, the earth, the animals, even the yellow hawkweeds and the bell-shaped multicolored gilias that he would caution against picking. "Leave them be," he'd say as a serious little boy. "The Creator gave them to everybody, not just to the one who picks them."

"Johnny," Valerie asked softly, "what do you really think of all this?"

He looked deeply worried and that bothered her

more than anything. Johnny was not easily disturbed. He was one to be calm, even lighthearted in times of difficulty. He was one who tried to cheer up everyone else. "I'm not sure, but I'm afraid something is awfully wrong. The teachers would come if they could."

Valerie licked her suddenly dry lips. "Do you think something has happened to them?"

"Yes. I'm afraid so. And whoever . . . well, whoever made sure that the teachers didn't come today also kept Ken and me from crossing the bridge. I'm afraid it's some crazy guys who maybe took over the school last night, waited for the teachers this morning, did something to them. Maybe they're on some trip—you know, high on drugs or something."

"You don't think Mr. Ainsley will come this afternoon?"

"They probably stopped him too." Johnny glanced up at the sky, which was totally blue and silent. "I haven't even seen any planes today."

"We aren't on a regular air route," Valerie said, growing cold inside.

"I know, but a few guys from around the valley usually take their planes up for a little spin in this kind of weather."

"That doesn't necessarily mean anything."

"No, it doesn't."

"What are you trying to say, Johnny? That the world has stopped or something? I mean, if you went into

Cinder Creek right now—don't you think you'd find our dads mending fences as usual?"

"I hope I would, but I'm not so sure. Anyway, if the bus doesn't come as usual, then we'll know that our folks know something is wrong . . . and can't do anything about it."

"Johnny, that's impossible. Something couldn't have happened to the whole town."

"How many people live in Cinder Creek? Fifty-four, -five?" He reached instinctively for Valerie's hand and grasped it with unusual firmness. "Come on, let's go back to the others."

Some of the boys congregated again at the principal's door with Bennie, who was saying, "I thought there might be something in the chem lab to make a small explosive to blast this door open, but I couldn't find anything. I think if we got a four-by-four and used it like a battering ram—you know, all the guys behind it— then maybe we could bust down the door."

Johnny nodded quickly. "Good, let's try." He went to Room 1 to round up the others and found Charlie advancing another theory. "If some nuts have taken over, then I bet it's some of those militant creeps—your guys, Davis."

"That's idiotic," Hugh snapped. "Whoever heard of this town? Why would they pick it?"

"Way I heard," Charlie said, "one of those militant groups pressured the forestry department into hiring your old man, Davis. I guess that means they heard about us, all right."

Anger flamed in Hugh's eyes. "My father has a master's degree in chemistry and that's why he got the job, fathead!"

"Cool off," Sandra advised, resentment carefully controlled in her own brown eyes. "Let's not get to snapping at each other like animals in a cage."

Johnny cut in from the doorway, "We're going to try to bust down the principal's door with a four-by-four and we need every guy's muscle."

It was one-fifteen when they aimed the four-by-four at the oak door. Bennie counted and they rushed at it at once, pressing their collective weight behind the improvised battering ram. But the old door merely groaned under the assault.

"Isn't there any other way into there?" Charlie asked breathlessly, leaning back and trying to recover from the effort.

"It's an inside room, no windows, no other door," Ken said.

"How come the darn fire department allowed that?" Charlie asked indignantly.

"Because," Johnny told him patiently, "way back then the fire department didn't have the nice little rule book that it's got now."

"We've simply got to try again," Bennie declared. Once more they put the four-by-four into position. They failed again and Charlie pronounced the whole idea hopeless. "We're just gonna knock ourselves out, that's all. It was a dumb idea."

"What's a smart idea, Charlie?" Hugh asked him sharply.

Charlie shrugged. "I don't know. Maybe the school bus will come at three like always and all of this is for nothing."

"Don't be that soft in the head, Charlie," Hugh said.

"You don't know that it's not coming," Red said, siding with Charlie again. They had been friends since fourth grade.

"We've got to keep trying the door," Johnny decided. "Come on, you guys. There's a phone in that office. . . ."

On the fourth attempt Bennie heard a faint crackling sound as the hinges of the door finally began to pull away from the ancient wood. By this time the girls were gathered at the end of the hall watching with hope.

Margaret admired the way Bennie took command from time to time. She thought now as she had many times before that if she ever accepted a date with any of the boys around here, it would be with Bennie. Johnny was all right, but too much the strong, primitive male, anxious to overprotect girls. Ken Tillich was really a weakling at heart, putty in the hands of a selfish little fluff like Suzanne. Hugh was too hung up on the race thing. And Red and Charlie were, in Margaret's scornful opinion, total wastes.

"It's going," Bennie shouted. With an almost human cry of pain, the great door yielded, flying aside in a shower of wood splinters and dust. A cry of praise went up from the girls as Bennie led the way into the small office.

It was in perfect order, just as Mr. Farnsworth always left it. But the battery-operated radio was nowhere in sight and a quick search did not turn it up.

The old black phone sat on the corner of the desk in its usual place and Bennie grabbed the receiver, clamping it eagerly to his ear, almost knocking his glasses off in the quick motion. But disappointment quickly stole the elation from his face. "No dial tone."

Johnny checked the outlet behind the desk. "Seems all right."

Bennie's eyes narrowed. "Must be that all the phones are dead, like the electricity. Must be something at the main wires. . . ."

Danielle heard that and she whirled around in the hallway and ran, her crying becoming a deafening scream. Gayle took off after her, panting. She couldn't keep up as the slim girl fled across the schoolyard and headed out into open country where only an occasional yucca stabbed the gray monotony of undulating sand.

It was Johnny, sprinting past Gayle, who caught up

29

to the hysterical girl. "Dany, come on," he said sharply, grasping her arm. "It's okay, don't take on like that. It's okay, come on now." But she continued to scream and tried to wrench free of him. "Stop it!" he shouted into her face, hoping to shock her back to her senses. But her hysteria increased until the open palm of his hand smartly struck her cheek. Her scream ended with a startled whimper.

Gayle reached the place and failed to understand why he had to strike her. "Don't hurt her!" Gayle shouted, her chubby body bathed in perspiration. After the words were out, she quickly put her fingers to her lips. Johnny looked at her in mild surprise. But he said nothing.

Bennie reached the scene, saying crisply to Gayle, "He had to do something." Margaret added with equal curtness, "Of course he did."

Gayle avoided Johnny's eyes, going to comfort Danielle who was sniffling softly now.

It was two in the afternoon and a sudden breeze turned chill as it passed over the snow on distant purple-shadowed mountains.

"Let's get back to the school," Suzanne said crossly, "whatever miserable good that will do." She carefully smoothed back her velvet dark hair, even now conscious of her appearance. "I wonder what my silly grandfather is doing right now. Whatever stupid, awful thing has happened, I hope he's satisfied, him and my parents who stuck me in this place while they went over to solve the problems in outer Tasmania or wherever!"

"The way I figure it," Johnny said, "we'll wait for dark and then go across the bridge and find out what happened."

"The bus might come," Janet said numbly, still clinging to a hope she didn't really believe in any more. Nobody else believed it, either.

Hugh glanced at the mountains surrounding the small valley on all sides but one, the narrow divide where Cinder Creek cut through. The mountains were not terribly steep, but they were a tangle of wild, twisting canyons. If someone were to try to hike out through the mountains, he'd have to cross some twenty miles of dangerous wilderness. The nearest town was Carson Corners, an even smaller place than Cinder Creek.

It was two-fifteen when they reached the school, and growing colder by the minute. Everybody went inside, choosing the friends they had before the nightmare began. Suzanne and Janet paired off in a corner of Room 1, where they exchanged resentful words about Cinder Creek. "When this stupid thing is over, I don't even think I'll wait for graduation," Suzanne said. "I'll just leave. I mean, what good will knowledge of the details of the French Revolution do me when I plan to be a folk singer?"

"Oh Suzy," Janet said, "if only I could come too!

Do you know that the closest I've ever been to a big town was once when I went to Phoenix?" Janet's father was a veterinarian, content in this nowhere valley. Janet felt that the whole wonderful, exciting world lay out there while she was shut up in this horrible place with cattle and brush rabbits and endless sweeping sand flowing to chocolate mountains. Like her, nothing went anywhere.

"Well, perhaps you could come with me. Do you have any money saved?"

"A little. Maybe two hundred dollars. Daddy has been after me to buy a heifer with it and enter it in the county fair this summer, but, wow, I'm about as interested in doing that as I'd be in baking a gooseberry pie and competing for first prize with your grandmother."

Suzanne laughed coldly. "Well, I've got a couple hundred saved too. We could thumb our way for a while, hitch a ride with some out-of-towner, maybe to Flagstaff or Yuma or anywhere, and then catch a bus, maybe to Los Angeles or San Francisco. If I auditioned I'm sure I could get into a coffeehouse, and maybe you could be a waitress."

"Oh Suzy!" Janet's eyes widened. "That would be so neat."

In another corner of the room, Charlie and Red speculated on what was going on. Charlie said, "I seen this science fiction movie once and everything was real quiet and deserted and this guy couldn't figure it out and then he sees like this big insect of some kind coming down the road and it turns out the whole town's been devoured by monster insects, like grasshoppers. . . ."

Red grimaced. "Aw, that's just a story."

"Yeah, but like what's happened to them—the teachers and old Farny? You know he's not somewhere drinking his afternoon tea."

"Maybe they're dead," Red said in a hollow voice. "Farny and the others." He shrugged then. "Naw, they couldn't be."

"Why not?" Charlie asked. "Why couldn't they be—why not, Red?"

"I don't know, Charlie. Hey, let's not talk about it, okay?"

In Room 2, Danielle and Gayle sat together in silence. Danielle remained dazed from her outburst, and Gayle was afraid to say anything that might start another spell of hysteria.

Margaret and the other girls talked while Bennie stood by the window watching the road where every afternoon at three o'clock, since before Bennie was born, Horace Ainsley had driven up in the big yellow bus. The last part of the journey was downhill, and Mr. Ainsley always remarked that it was slightly dangerous. It was straight and steep so it was necessary to take it all in low gear. "Less'n we want to go outta control and highball down past the old schoolhouse," Mr. Ainsley would say, "and go crashing into Strawberry Rock." A huge boulder at the end of the dead-end road had been named Strawberry Rock for its rosy glow. Mr. Ainsley was proud of his driving record, almost forty years without an accident unless you counted the time a flock of chickens got in front of him and he scattered a few feathers.

"It's almost three," Margaret declared, shattering what had been a long silence.

"It's coming—the bus is coming," Bennie gasped, and they all crowded to the windows. Yes, there it was. But something was different—the speed of the yellow bus. Mr. Ainsley never drove like that. It was as if a maniac were at the wheel the way the big old bus was hurtling toward the school stop.

4. The Fire

"She's highballing," Hugh shouted.

Johnny gasped. "Not even slowing down."

"It isn't going to stop——" Bennie's voice was taut.

The bus went by, slowing a bit as the downgrade lessened. But the impact with Strawberry Rock was inevitable.

There was a deafening crash, the sound of shattering glass, seats flying from their underpinnings. Then silence.

"I'm going down to look," Johnny said, and the others followed, strung out in a long line behind him. Nobody said a word.

They approached the bus cautiously. Sand was blowing around the wheels and the wind whistled through the open, shattered windows. The accordion doors were bent and hanging. Johnny peered in at Mr. Ainsley's empty seat, then his eyes moved to the steering wheel. A piece of scrap metal wedged the wheel into one position, obviously placed there by someone who wanted the bus to keep on a straight course.

"They must have started her at the top of the grade and just let her go, gathering her own momentum," Johnny said. His voice was dry and flat. He drew his hands into fists, pounding them uselessly against his hard thighs. He kicked the wrecked bus and the sound echoed like a dull protest.

"It seems to be," Margaret pronounced gravely, her narrow, bespectacled eyes on the yellow bus, "a diabolical, carefully conceived plot."

"It doesn't make sense," Ken said, his face pale. "It's like we are all on some wild trip and pretty soon we'll wake up and tell each other what crazy nightmares we had."

"But we're all having the same nightmare," Bennie pointed out.

Danielle had been calm about the bus crash. Now she joined the cluster standing around the wreckage and said in an almost normal voice, "Maybe it is a dream, like not really happening. We can't all be here like this, not really. I think that very soon I'm going to wake up and be glad it's all over." She looked hopefully at Ken, her thin, drawn face marked by the dark circles under her eyes.

In one sense, Danielle's entire life had been a strange

dream, a nightmare from which she had been constantly waiting to awaken. Her parents' angry quarrels, then the divorce two years ago. Danielle had lived in France for a year with her mother and an artist stepfather, but it hadn't been fun or romantic or anything like the way it sounded. The new husband hated her for some obscure reason and so it was decided that Danielle should go live with her father. They were almost strangers, and the girl was frightened. Her father seemed equally frightened, and they coexisted in the house like anxious shadows hurrying their separate ways, trying desperately to avoid a confrontation with one another.

"They wish to frighten us," Margaret deduced, discussing their predicament as though it were of no more personal consequence to her than a piece of news heard on the radio. Margaret prided herself on being practical and down to earth, whatever happened.

"They're doing just fine," Johnny commented grimly. "Let's go back to the school. There's nowhere else to go."

In another few hours a pale circle of moon appeared in the sky, like a chalk-drawn zero, but there was still plenty of daylight left. It was four-thirty.

Hugh said, "Our parents know by now that we aren't coming home." He could picture his mother, a slight, pretty brown woman, much like Sandra, but loving her family with such intensity that she'd panic at something like this. He could see his father, fear in his own eyes, trying to calm her. Or wasn't that the way it was happening at all? Were his parents incapable of being concerned because something terrible had happened to them? The thought of that was like the slam of a hard blow against Hugh's chest.

Suzanne laughed, a forced, strained sound. "Of course they know we're not coming home. Our dear relatives know their precious children aren't home—but you don't see them coming here, trembling and full of concern, do you? Maybe they're relieved. Grandmother never gets tired of telling me what an awful burden children are. 'First you bear them in pain, then you raise them in trouble and in the end they're the worst grief of all because they usually disappoint you.' If she's said that once, she's said it a thousand times. Maybe now she thinks, 'Wow, little Suzy just disappeared—how about that?'"

"You don't believe that," Janet said in a small voice. She did not get along that well with her parents, but she knew they would be terribly concerned if they thought something had happened to her. Suzanne shrugged her shoulders, but all at once there were tears in her eyes. "If they cared that much about me—any of them—would my parents just dump me and go running off to some foreign country? And my grandparents, they're old. They don't want a kid at this stage of the game. Wow, my grandfather is seventy years old. If I play some music I like, he gets up and runs into the other room and slams the door like the music is going to kill him or something."

Ken became suddenly protective. "Suzy, don't cry."

Suzanne quickly recovered from her sudden panic. "I'm not crying. Are you crazy or something? What's to cry about—them? I knew they never cared about me, any of them. I should cry about it now! What do you think I am, a sentimental idiot?"

Valerie looked at her watch. On an ordinary day she would have been home for almost half an hour now. She would probably be helping her younger sister, Bobbie, with her homework. Bobbie attended the elementary school on the outskirts of town with only about four other kids. "I hope Bobbie isn't scared," she said aloud.

Johnny looked at her sympathetically. "I'm sure our families are okay, Val."

"You sure, huh?" Charlie asked. "Well, if they're okay—if my old man is sitting in the kitchen drinking coffee as usual, why don't he wonder where I am?"

Johnny tried to change the subject. "Listen, you guys, a couple of us are going to have to try to cross that bridge when it gets dark. Who's going with me?"

"Me," Hugh said promptly. "I blend in great with the night." Nobody laughed. Silently, Johnny and Hugh headed out for the bridge.

39

Slowly, as the sun went down, the others walked back to the school and gathered in Room 1. "I've never been here all night. Never," Red said.

"None of us have," Bennie answered.

"I bet it's spooky," Red continued. "I bet coyotes howl like crazy out here at night."

"They howl all over the valley," Margaret pointed out. "I'm sure that isn't going to scare anybody."

Charlie turned to her angrily. "Man, don't nuthin' bother you? You're really weird, Illiam."

"I'm simply a rational person and the prospect of some coyotes howling doesn't send me into hysterics," Margaret said. "I'm sorry if that threatens your male ego, Gilman."

"Man, no wonder no guy gives you a second look," Charlie told her cruelly.

Margaret blinked at the blow, but landed quickly on her feet. "Oh, Gilman, do you honestly think that I lie awake nights dreaming of the possibility of being courted by some brainless goof like you?"

Bennie Bryce's mouth widened in a swift, passing smile. He had to admire Margaret's spunk. It was something to see.

"It will be dinnertime pretty soon at home," Gayle said to nobody in particular. "We were having ham tonight. And pineapple."

"I got a sandwich left from lunch if you want it," Danielle said in a momentary return to reality.

40

"No thanks," Gayle said. "I couldn't get anything down my throat."

"I sure could," Charlie said. "I'm starving."

Danielle handed the sandwich to Charlie. "It's sort of stale, by now. It's Swiss cheese."

"That's okay, I don't mind," Charlie said, taking the sandwich and unwrapping it quickly.

Ken stood by the window, staring out unseeingly. He wished fervently he were back in Van Nuys. He would probably be making the papers with his sports feats and have all the pretty girls competing for his attention. He had surfed a lot when he lived in Van Nuys, cutting through the canyons to Malibu every weekend. Of course Ken and his brothers did enjoy the ranch, riding horses, that sort of thing, and Ken figured he could eventually win Suzanne. But just now, staring into the ominous darkness, he wished he were back home where something like this couldn't happen.

It was then, as he looked south, that Ken saw the dull red glow spreading in the sky. Johnny and Hugh had been gone for little more than ten minutes. At first glance, Ken thought it was the afterglow of sunset, but the direction was wrong.

"Hey, Bennie," he called softly, and the other boy joined him at the window.

"A fire!" Bennie whispered, shocked. Ken's heart was pounding wildly. His arms and legs felt numb. "The town, do you think, Bennie?"

Bennie shook his head. "I don't think so . . . it looks closer than town. Can't be more than a mile and a half off."

"A brush fire maybe," Ken said hopefully.

"Maybe."

"Hey, Bennie." Ken's voice was low and shaky. "I'm really scared. I don't mind saying it, this thing is really getting to me. If we knew what was happening, we could deal with it—but, man, what's out there? Is the rest of the world out there or did something happen———?"

"Sure, the rest of the world is out there," Bennie said. "Look up—the old moon is hanging there as usual, and I heard coyotes a minute ago. If we were in Phoenix right now, we'd see a million neon lights and hear horns honking and smell auto exhaust on the crowded streets . . ."

"Oh, Lord," Ken gasped, "I wish I were there. I wish I were anywhere but here." Bennie turned and looked at the other boy in some surprise.

Ken Tillich was a big, muscular guy, the all-American type. He was wide-eyed and handsome, carved from the traditional stuff of heroes. But he was really a very weak person, Bennie realized with something of a shock. "Come on, Ken. Let's not fall apart, okay?"

"Bennie, I think we ought to just hike out of here anyway we can. Just head for the nearest settlement."

Ken wiped the perspiration off his face. "I mean, if the guys don't make it—if the fire means . . ."

"The nearest settlement is Carson Corners. Maybe twelve people live there, and it's a good stiff hike even for somebody experienced."

"And whatever happened in Cinder Creek maybe happened to them too . . ."

"We don't know that anything happened in Cinder Creek," Bennie said with little conviction.

"Yes, we do. If our parents were okay, they'd be here."

Bennie said nothing. He watched the fire grow larger, then burn with a consistent glow.

Suzanne joined them at the window. "Something is burning south of here!"

Bennie turned to her. "Shhh." He didn't want Danielle to hear, but it was too late.

She jumped up. "What's burning?"

"Just a little brush, Dany, nothing to get excited about."

But Red McGinnis got up as well and came to the window, "Wow, it's a big fire—hey, you guys, a big fire!"

"We know it," Margaret said.

"And you're just sitting there? Boy, you're something else!" Charlie joined Red at the window. "Maybe they got one of those death-ray guns and they just evaporated the guys."

43

"Oh, you stupid idiot," Margaret exploded. "What kind of a thing is that to say? If you'd read your textbooks instead of science fiction comic books, maybe you'd have better than a D average!"

"D average?" Charlie shouted. "What difference does any of that stuff make now? You crazy or something?"

"Oh, Charlie," Margaret said, "next week at this time everything will be back to normal." She said that mostly for the benefit of Sandra and Valerie. The boys out there near the bridge were very special to those two.

"It's the bridge," Suzanne concluded. "The bridge is burning."

"Yes," Margaret agreed, "I think so."

"Maybe the boys got across before——" Sandra said.

Margaret frowned. "Maybe." But her eyes doubted it.

Suzanne made no pretense. "Of course they didn't get across. Why should we fool ourselves? Whoever is out there made very sure of that. It's almost as if they know exactly what we're doing."

Red glanced up at the vents in the room. "You think they got this place bugged or something?"

"It's possible," Bennie said. "They could have easily installed listening devices."

"Wouldn't we see them?" Charlie asked.

"No, not necessarily," Bennie told him. "They could

be rigged up to the regular PA system, concealed some-way."

"That's true," Margaret added. "An expert in that sort of thing could do it easily. Why even *I* have fooled around with radios, and I helped my father build a television set when I was twelve."

Charlie glared at Margaret. "Your old man is some kind of crazy scientist, isn't he?"

Margaret sniffed. "He's a senior chemist for the forestry service. If that makes him a 'crazy scientist'—well, have it your own way."

"Who knows what kinds of things those guys are up to? Like that Dr. Frankenstein—he was a scientist, and he was a monster, too," Charlie muttered.

"Charlie," Margaret said scornfully, "Dr. Franken-stein was a fictional character and he *wasn't* a monster. Anyway, if you want to believe my father builds an-droids in his spare time, then just go right ahead and believe it!"

"The fire is going down a little," Ken observed.

"Probably there's nothing left to burn," Suzanne said dismally.

Valerie struggled against tears as she stared into the darkness at the diminishing red glow. *Please God, make them come back all right . . . please!* Her lips barely moved.

5. The Breakout

Hugh and Johnny paused on the last rise before descending to Cinder Creek and the bridge. The fire was a wild inferno, voraciously consuming the old wooden underpinnings of the structure, licking rapidly through the dry, brittle planks. Flaming pieces of wood dropped into the white water, continuing to burn for a few moments until the charred object drowned in the undertow. For a few seconds the entire outline of the doomed bridge was alive with dancing flames, almost like an elaborate fireworks display. It was an eerie sight against the totally black sky.

"I don't see anybody around," Hugh said in a dull voice.

Johnny shook his head. "But they're out there. They must be." His eyes searched the rocky outcroppings on both sides of the bridge for some shadow, some shape, but there was nothing but exploding sparks.

"Johnny, what about their timing? I mean, why didn't they burn down the bridge a couple of hours ago? Why just before we got to it—like they knew and wanted to impress us."

"Maybe they've got a way of knowing what goes on in that school," Johnny said.

Hugh laughed mirthlessly. "You know, man, this morning I was wondering if I'd get that art scholarship to a college in Los Angeles. I was all angry and worried that maybe those white cats in admissions wouldn't let a guy like me in."

Johnny turned, "Art? I never even knew you were interested in art."

Hugh shrugged, "I haven't spread the word around. Even my parents are against it, but it's what I want to do. Last summer I took a class in Phoenix and my teacher said I had ability. . . . Funny though, all of a sudden none of it seems real or important—or anything. The only thing I can think about now is getting home, seeing my folks again and, you know. . . ."

"I know," Johnny said softly, touching the other boy's arm gently in the darkness.

When Johnny came into view, Valerie's emotions burst. She ran toward him, tumbling into his arms, crying freely. "Hey, hey," he said, putting his arms around her. "Hey, quit it, will you, girl?" He smiled a little and drew her away from him, at arm's length. "It's okay. Okay."

"The bridge is gone," Hugh announced flatly. "I guess you figured that out for yourselves."

"Where does that leave us?" Ken asked, his voice shaking again.

Hugh shrugged. "The maddening thing is they seemed to know we were coming before we got there."

Suzanne said, "We were wondering about the same thing. Do you think the school might be bugged? Bennie and Margaret said it would be an easy thing to do."

Johnny glanced up at the loudspeaker. "I'll bet that's it."

Margaret turned to stare at the speaker. "I suppose they will contact us sooner or later and tell us what they want."

"Yeah?" Charlie said. "You think so, huh?" Something was coming alive in his mind, some suspicion that, once born, grew rapidly, and Margaret was the focus of it.

But Margaret continued in her even voice, her brown eyes magnified as usual behind her thick glasses, giving her a strange, disproportionate look.

"You maybe know something about all this that we don't know, huh, Illiam?" Charlie's voice was belligerent now and his eyes glowed angrily.

"What?"

"You been pretty cool all through this, like maybe you know what's coming off," Charlie said.

"Don't be a fool, Charlie," Sandra cut in. "Maggie is just as worried as the rest of us. She just happens to have better self-control."

"Listen!" Charlie's eyes continued to glow. "I never liked some of the creeps Illiam hung around with last summer."

Margaret laughed contemptuously. "Do you mean those nice young people who visited me from Phoenix?"

"Yeah, you can call them nice if you want to, but they didn't look too nice to me. Or to my folks neither. They were real weirdo types with Indian headbands and crazy ideas. I saw you all sitting in a circle one night making wild moves with your bodies, like——" His breath came now in quick, excited rasps. "I told my old man about it, and he said maybe you're devil worshipers or something."

"We were doing yoga exercises, you simpleton. All of those kids were just nice young people who share my concern with issues like air pollution and peace and women's liberation."

"I'm not so sure about that. I say maybe they were all nuts and you're some kind of nut too, Illiam. And maybe you're in on whatever's happening to us!"

"Why don't you quit, Gilman," Hugh said with disgust.

49

"You shut your fat mouth, Davis," Charlie yelled back, and Hugh made an angry move toward him.

Johnny stepped between them, "We can't afford something like this."

"I'd just like to look into Illiam's locker," Charlie said, "I'd like to see what she's got in there."

Margaret looked amazed. "Are you really serious? Are you really and truly serious?"

"Yeah, I'm serious. I'm just wondering if we might find some proof in your locker."

"I wouldn't open my locker for you, Charlie Gilman, if you begged me on your hands and knees," Margaret told him angrily, "and I consider it beneath contempt that you would even suggest such a thing!"

"Yeah?" Now Red McGinnis sided with Charlie. "Well, if you've got nothing to hide, then how come you won't let us look inside your locker?"

Ken watched the confrontation with surprise and horror. He had never suspected that any of the thirteen could be involved in this terrible thing that had happened. He wasn't ready to believe Charlie's accusation, but he did wonder why Margaret wasn't willing to open her locker and prove Charlie wrong. Ken would have opened his locker in a moment if anyone had suspected him of anything. Now he stared at Margaret in worried confusion and half believed she did have something to hide.

The lockers were in the hall between Rooms 1 and

2. There were fifty lockers, but only fifteen had been used in the past ten years. Danielle Frazer walked to Margaret's locker and looked at it with puzzled interest. "What do you have in your locker, Maggie? Why won't you open it and show us what you have in there? Please, Maggie."

Margaret gave her a superior look. "I will not let a boob like Gilman make some preposterous charge and then allow myself to be treated like a common criminal."

Charlie stood a few feet behind Margaret. "You better open it up, Illiam, or I'll bust it open myself."

"You just try!" Margaret cried in a high-pitched voice.

"Hey!" Johnny moved closer. "Let's stop this nonsense. Listen, Maggie, we all know that Charlie is off his rocker to suspect you of anything, but why don't you let him look in your locker just for the sake of peace? I mean, humor him."

"Yeah." Ken added his encouragement, forcing his lips into a weak smile. "You can prove just how ridiculous Charlie is acting. You can prove it so easily, Maggie."

Suzanne glanced at Janet and whispered, "I'll bet she *does* have something to hide. I always thought she was strange. She's a loner and that's the kind you have to watch. I read that once in a magazine article." It suddenly made perfect sense to Suzanne. Strange, un-

51

naturally brilliant, unattractive Margaret Illiam might just be part of this terrible nightmare. Why, she might even be the brains behind it.

"There is a principle at stake here," Margaret declared, almost reveling in her persecution now. "I shall not yield." The real danger that confronted them all was forgotten for the moment.

"Open the damn thing and let them have their look," Johnny snapped, exasperated now.

"Yeah," Hugh put in, "go on, Maggie, open it! Open up your personal possessions so Charlie can paw through everything. Never mind your dignity." His voice oozed with sarcasm.

"You just want to make trouble, don't you, Davis?" Charlie accused hotly. He whirled around. "I'm getting me a shovel, and if that locker isn't open when I come back, I'm gonna bust it wide open!"

Margaret moved in front of her locker. "You're not opening my locker and that's final!"

Charlie reached out suddenly, grabbing Margaret's shoulder and trying to shove her aside. But another hand came down on Charlie's shoulder. "Don't manhandle her, Charlie," Bennie advised coldly.

Charlie spun around, infuriated. "Don't you mix in this, Bryce—you're not built for it!"

Bennie disregarded the slur on his size. "Just leave her alone, Charlie. She has her rights. It's like Hugh said, a matter of dignity. We ought to be ashamed of ourselves for allowing our predicament to turn us into savages."

When Charlie again tried to push Margaret aside, Bennie gave him a hard shove. Bennie was pale with anger. Charlie turned and violently knocked Bennie aside, toppling him off his feet. "Any other comers?" Charlie demanded, his fists swinging before him menacingly.

Hugh stared at the heavy boy for a moment and his mind hurtled backward to an elementary school in a small rural town. Sandra had been suspected of stealing money from the teacher's desk; she hadn't done it of course, but they had made her open her tiny red patent leather purse and she had cried torrents. She had been only six, but when Hugh had found her sobbing in the schoolyard, he had wanted to bust somebody good. It all came back, and he advanced on Charlie. "Yeah, I'll take you on, Gilman, with pleasure."

But Johnny's voice interceded. "I won't let this go on. Maggie——"

Margaret exhaled with disgust. "Oh *all right*—just to prevent violence——" She turned to her locker, spun the dial and opened it. Charlie crowded in for a look and immediately shouted, "Here it is—here's the bug!" He turned holding the device aloft. "See, what'd I tell you? She's in on it—she's working with them against us!"

"Oh Gilman!" Margaret laughed caustically. "You'd

have been great at the Salem witch trials. That happens to be a toy slide projector that was a gift from my little cousin in Tucson."

Johnny took the device from Charlie. "I think you owe Maggie an apology."

The locker contained books, a record album, nothing else. Charlie's face turned red, but he said nothing.

"I wouldn't accept his apology anyway," Margaret said, "although actually I pity him. They say we show our true natures in times of crisis and Charlie is certainly a pitiable little person." She turned to Bennie. "I just want you to know that I think you were marvelous."

"Marvelous for falling down?" Bennie asked with a wry look.

"No," Margaret said solemnly, "marvelous for standing up to injustice." She smiled toward Hugh then, and he gave a crooked smile in return.

Back in Room 1, Johnny and Ken took down maps of the region and began to plan the hike out toward Carson Corners. "Tomorrow, with first light," Johnny said. "The map here marks the trail we can take."

"What do we do meantime?" Gayle asked.

"Get some sleep, I guess," Hugh suggested. He sat down at one of the desks and put his head down on it, setting the example.

"I could never sleep," Gayle protested, but after a

moment she sat down, too, and one by one most of the others followed.

Johnny touched Val's arm and motioned for her to come outside with him.

They walked several yards from the school before Johnny stopped. "Val, I'm sure the school is bugged."

Valerie's eyes widened. "But you explained our plans to——" Then she understood. "Oh, I see. You want them to think we're going to Carson Corners tomorrow morning."

"Right. Ken and I will be heading for Cinder Creek again as soon as the others are asleep. We're both strong and we're pretty good swimmers if need be. There's a small boat in the reeds this side of the creek, and we'll try to make it across in that. I figure they'll be expecting us to stay put until morning so maybe they won't be watching the creek too closely. Listen, Val, when the others wake up, just tell them Ken and I decided to head for Carson Corners by ourselves, that we figured it would be safer for the others to stay where they are. It isn't that I don't trust the other kids, but if anybody knows, then they might blurt it out and tip whoever is listening."

Valerie looked worriedly at him. "Oh Johnny—that means you and Ken will be facing whatever it is in town. . . ."

"We'll take it slow and easy, Val. There's no other way. We've got to find out what's happening." He tried to smile. "Hey, don't look so sad. If you promise not to look so sad, I'll take you to the prom."

Valerie smiled weakly. They had made plans to go to the prom together a long time ago. It had been last summer, one night when they looked at each other and seemed to realize, both at once, that they were not children any more. Valerie understood then that the strong but gentle boy who'd been her sturdy playmate was now a handsome young man who set her heart to racing, and he noticed that the little tomboy he'd taught to ride and climb as well as himself had come to be a lovely young woman, inspiring in him a great tenderness.

In Room 1, Red crawled over to a corner, wrapped his coat around himself and went to sleep. The others who were not in on the secret were sound asleep, too. All but Ken, whose face remained silvery with perspiration. He looked so sick with fear that he seemed near vomiting.

When it was close to midnight, Valerie watched Johnny and Ken move like shadows from the room and out into the night.

Outside, Johnny said, "I told Valerie what we were doing. I wanted somebody to know and I trust her not to blurt it out."

"Yeah." Ken dried off his face with his handkerchief. The most dangerous thing that had ever happened to him in his life was when a slow-moving car had struck him while he was riding his bicycle. He remembered the day as if it were yesterday, although he had been only seven at the time. He remembered seeing the grillwork of the car like the grinning teeth of a wild animal. He remembered the awful sensation of hitting the street and lying there, screaming, with dozens of concerned, strange faces hovering over him. A policeman had come finally, a red-faced, tough-sounding policeman. "It's okay, boy, you ain't hurt that bad. Just a busted leg." But Ken had continued to scream and cry until the ambulance came and he was sedated. It didn't matter that the policeman kept telling him to be a "little man"—he was hurt and gut-scared and he couldn't be a little man for anybody. He was ashamed of it afterward, but he couldn't help it at the time. Not any more than now he could help the stream of perspiration coursing down his face and body.

The moon had gone behind some clouds as the boys moved swiftly down the road toward the creek. "What if they found the boat and sunk it?" Ken asked.

"I doubt it. It was hidden in the reeds. Nobody would know it was even there unless they lived around here."

As the boys came down to the creek, they could see the bridge, one large piece remaining, dipping into the water like the skeleton of a monster, cold and dead. They moved slowly through the coarse grass with the hollow jointed stems. Many times Johnny had come here, broken off a stem and blown through it or peered through it like through a telescope.

"There's the boat," Johnny whispered, making out its bulk at water's edge. They went knee-deep in water and examined the tiny craft, finding it sturdy enough.

Johnny took out a pocketknife and sawed the rope that moored it to a stump. "You want to get in first, Ken? I'll hold her steady." Ken nodded, crawling awkwardly into the boat, stifling a gasp when it wobbled. He hated himself for feeling like this. He had surfed, tumbling joyfully around in the waves, back home, but somehow his stomach was twisted into icy knots now and everything terrified him. He sat down quickly in the boat and Johnny jumped in. Ken looked at Johnny and quietly envied him his abundance of courage.

Johnny grasped the oars and began pushing away from shore. The boat creaked as it was roused from its familiar place, then glided slowly into the placid waters. "So far, so good," Johnny said.

Ken dipped his hand in the water, "Wow, that's cold. I hope we don't end up swimming."

The small craft began to rock as the fast currents began, and Ken gripped the side nearest him, his lips whitening as he pressed them together. Johnny continued to row, fighting the heaving water. "Give me a hand here, Ken," he gasped, and Ken helped to push the blades against the violent water. But the boat rolled and tumbled precariously. The water seemed to have gained the upper hand. Ken's face went as white as the foaming water. "Johnny—we can't make it! We'll drown! The water's too rough——"

"We've got to make it," Johnny shot back. "We're in the middle of the rapids now and it's no easier going back! Ken—help me!"

The rapids began to toss the boat capriciously, like a toy hurtling down a rain-swollen storm drain. They almost overturned twice. Ken screamed, "We have to turn back!" He was almost out of his mind with terror, with thoughts of the black waters closing over his face. It was as if the years had disappeared and he was a small boy again staring into the advancing silver teeth of a Chevy sedan, screaming as the bone in his leg cracked. "Johnny!" He was sobbing, blind with panic. And the boat pitched again with malicious frenzy.

6. Dany Disappears

"Shut up and help me!" Johnny shouted. Ken began pushing the oar against the turbulent creek. And then, after one last terrible heave, the waters quieted and they were through the white water and nearing the opposite shore.

Ken leaned back and shook convulsively. He watched now with desperate envy as the Cherokee continued to row, quiet, composed. The boat bounced into shallow water and Johnny threw the tow rope around a sapling. The boys crawled from the craft and waded up to their knees, then climbed onto the marshy shore.

"I'm sorry, Johnny. I acted like a fool," Ken apologized.

"Forget it," Johnny told him. "It was a bad few minutes."

They moved up a small hill. From the summit they

knew they could see some of the ranches stretching across the broad valley. Enticed by the hope of seeing reassuring lights glowing softly, the boys hurried. But when they reached the top, they saw only darkness.

Johnny pointed. "The Halstead ranch should be right over there. We ought to see their lights."

"Maybe they don't burn a night light," Ken said. "You know, they're old, probably short of money, trying to save."

"Yeah, maybe. Come on, let's find out," Johnny said and led the way down the hill, past some ancient cottonwoods, the steady hum of the night wind at his back.

They spotted the Halstead windmill etched on the night sky, lazily moving with the currents. They saw the outline of the old well in the front yard and the gate. Johnny and Ken went through the swinging gate and up to the front door.

"We'll probably scare them half to death coming at this hour," Ken suggested, but Johnny said nothing. He pressed the doorbell and waited. "Maybe the bell doesn't work," Ken said, and Johnny hit the wood frame of the door with his knuckles.

"Hey, Mr. Halstead. It's Johnny Harrison out here," Johnny shouted. But no response came. His hand lowered to the doorknob, and when he turned it, it yielded immediately. A sick feeling shot through his body. It wasn't right that the door should be unlocked. He opened it slowly. "Hey, anybody home?" But there was really no need to ask. Everything about the house screamed of emptiness.

Ken tried the light switch. There was a clicking sound, but no light. Obviously the main town generator was out. Johnny slipped his flashlight from his belt strap and played the yellow beam around the room. Everything was in precise order. Mrs. Halstead's knitting still lay on a chair, the two needles sticking out of the yarn expectantly, as if the woman had left her work for only a moment. Mr. Halstead's pipe rested on the table by the phone as if he'd laid it down to answer a call.

Johnny went to the phone, picked it up and listened to a profound silence. He did not even bother to go into the other rooms. His eyes moved across the living room to a large clock. The time was 9:01. The clock had stopped at that hour. That, Johnny figured, was when everything had stopped.

Ken wiped the sweat off his upper lip. "The Quantrain ranch is next, isn't it?"

"Yeah, let's go," Johnny said, walking quickly as if he wanted to be out of the house as swiftly as possible.

"What if . . . it's the same thing there. . . ."

"The people couldn't have all disappeared."

"I was reading the other day in some newspaper about how this gang of maniacs went through a

62

house, wiping out everybody, one by one. Something like eight in the end."

"Don't think about it, okay?"

It was a hard two-mile walk to the Quantrain ranch. By the time they reached the outer fence, it was almost three in the morning. The front gate, usually locked, stood open, moving slightly back and forth in the wind. The Quantrain's police dog was nowhere in sight. The boys moved carefully through the gate to the front door and, as was the case at the Halstead house, the doorbell brought no response. Johnny's hand went to the doorknob and turned it reluctantly. He moved inside and mechanically but to no avail tried the light switch. The phone was dead. It was all very thorough. The living-room clock had stopped at 9:01.

They checked through the rooms, one by one this time. There was nothing to suggest even the slightest struggle. The people were just simply gone. The boys went outside to check the corrals where three bay horses were kept. The corral gate was open and the horses were gone.

Suddenly a sick look washed through Johnny's eyes. Lying about thirty feet away was the body of the police dog, shot through the head.

"He was probably attacking them, whoever they were. He was about as good a watchdog as I've ever seen, Ken."

"What do we do now, Johnny?" Ken asked in despair.

"Go from ranch to ranch finding empty houses and dead animals?"

"We've got no choice. Somewhere we'll find somebody and then we'll know. Let's look in the garage and see if the pickup is there. I could hot-wire it." But when they opened the garage door, they found that the truck was gone. "Okay," Johnny said, "we keep walking."

At four in the morning, Hugh stirred in Room 1. He noticed that Johnny and Ken were gone and announced the news loudly. Valerie said quickly, "It's all right. They decided to start early and go alone. They thought it was safer for the rest of us to stay here."

"That's mighty strange," Charlie said, rubbing the sleep from his eyes. "I mean, what's the big idea of sneaking off like that without saying anything?"

Red got up and limped to the window, stiff from sleeping on the floor. "It's getting sort of light. Wow, yesterday morning I had six hotcakes for breakfast. What I wouldn't do for a couple of them now."

"Yesterday I had a stack of pancakes a foot high and six link sausages," Charlie said. "And my dad was talking about selling a tractor to Amos Digby. I wonder if he ever got there."

Danielle woke up. "Have Johnny and Ken gone?"
Gayle nodded. "I guess so."
Danielle said slowly, "I wished they'd taken me too.

64

All night I wished. I wanted so much to leave. I don't want to stay here any more."

"Oh Dany," Margaret said, "you only would have held them back. They want to make the best time possible."

Danielle went to the window. Dawn was slowly coming alive. "I don't like it here. They'll find us here."

"Come on, Dany," Gayle said, "we can make it if we just stick together."

Danielle ignored her. "We'll go crazy just waiting for something to happen. I think that's what they want to do—to drive us crazy. I saw a movie once—the husband wanted to drive the wife crazy so he could have her put in a hospital and he could marry someone else. The husband kept making awful things happen and pretty soon the wife was crazy just like he wanted her to be. . . ."

"Please, Dany. Just sit down," Gayle pleaded, but Danielle remained at the window.

Margaret found some paper cups and a can of instant coffee in the principal's office. Most of them drank coffee in silence, and a few went outside to watch the red dawn spread its color assertively over the sky. It was five o'clock when they all gathered in Room 1 again. It was then that Gayle Cherneck said, "Where's Dany?"

"I saw her go outside," Suzanne said, "oh, about

thirty minutes ago. Said something about getting air, I think."

"Who saw her since then?" Bennie asked worriedly.

Charlie spoke up, "I think I saw her walking under the trees. She looked strange so I didn't bother her."

"I'll bet she tried to follow the boys," Margaret said.

"Which means she's walking into that dangerous canyon," Sandra cried. "Come on, we've got to catch up to her."

They all went outside and moved in the direction Danielle probably would have gone if she had intended to follow Johnny and Ken to Carson Corners. "Stupid little weirdo," Charlie complained. His feet already were hurting as he walked over the rough ground. "What did she do a fool thing like this for?"

"Because she was scared like the rest of us," Hugh said. He tried to find Danielle's footprints and occasionally he would see the rippled imprint of her tennis shoe, but then the tracks would disappear over a patch of hard rock.

When they reached the perimeter of the small valley, they began to shout. "Dany! Heyyy, Dany!" There was no answering sound, only a faint echo bouncing off the rocky summits.

"Let's us, a couple of guys, start up," Hugh said. "It's too steep for everybody." Bennie nodded and they began to climb the narrow, winding trail. They hadn't gotten a hundred yards when gunfire whistled past their heads. Both boys spun around and hurried back down the trail, out of firing range. "Somebody is up there in the rocks watching us," Hugh said breathlessly. "Obviously he's got a good view of this whole little valley."

Gayle's eyes widened. "But Dany must have gotten through—if they'd shot at Dany we'd have heard. . . ."

"Yeah, that *is* funny," Charlie admitted. "But maybe she was just lucky. Maybe they didn't see her."

"I doubt it," Bennie said gravely. "For some reason of their own, they must have let her through. Anyway, they aren't about to let us find out."

"They probably have Dany by now," Gayle said, her voice trembling. "Whoever, *what*ever, they are, they have poor Dany. . . ." She dropped her face in her hands and cried noisily as the group made its way slowly back to the school.

7. The Strangers

Johnny and Ken had reached two more ranches. In various places four watchdogs lay dead, and the farm animals had been scattered. It was the same in each house. The people were gone, and the items of their daily lives lay where they had left them. Other than the dead dogs, there were no signs of violence. What silent, deadly, efficient force had come this morning at 9:01 to insidiously subtract the people from this town?

The handsome Tillich ranch loomed in the distance, the rambling, roughhewn fence stretching between corrals. The Tillichs raised palomino horses. Johnny took a quick look at Ken's face and wondered whether he could stand seeing his own place struck by the same disaster they'd found in the other homes. "Hey, Ken, why don't you take a rest and let me look around?"

Ken shook his head. "My collie usually comes when I'm within a mile. I whistle and she comes. . . ." But he didn't have the heart to whistle, for he feared that this time—and forever after—she wouldn't come.

"She's pretty gentle," Johnny said. "Maybe they didn't need to . . . well, you know. The other dogs were watchdogs, German shepherds and Dobermans."

"She's smart too. Maybe she just took off for the hills," Ken said, trying to reassure himself.

They moved in closer and saw the ranch gate open. The palomino horses were nowhere to be seen, nor was the collie. Ken went silently to the door and turned the knob. "Oh my God, it's open," he whispered, in a way pleading for it to be somehow different here. But it was no different. The people—his people—were gone. Ken sat down in one of the living-room chairs and wept. He was not even ashamed that Johnny was standing there watching him. He said in a half sob, "It's worse when it's . . . your own place, Johnny. . . ."

"Yeah, sure," Johnny said hoarsely. He turned away and looked out the picture window that gave a sweeping view of the desert and the mountains, a deceptively peaceful view.

"My dad . . ." Ken began slowly, "my dad always wanted to get out of the rat race, always talking about it. He was so worried about the smog getting him. And about his ulcer—he must've drunk a million gallons of milk for his ulcer. It bugged me to leave the good old Malibu surf. I guess we argued about it a few times. . . ." His voice cracked as he continued, "And now . . . now I'd give the whole Pacific Ocean and the best surf God ever created to see my dad come through that hallway and go to the refrigerator and get a bottle of his damn milk. . . ."

"I know," Johnny said. "Listen, we better get going."

"Get going where? Where, Johnny? I can't take any more of it. I don't want to open any more unlocked doors and find any more empty houses or dead dogs."

"Ken, you can't just sit here."

"I can't go on either." A kind of desperate apathy gripped him. "I'm finished. Maybe it's the beginning of the end of the world. Maybe the world stopped at 9:01 yesterday morning and we thirteen were the only ones who forgot to die."

"Ken, you're talking crazy. . . ."

"Maybe. It doesn't matter anyway. I can't go on. This is the end of the line for me. I'm sorry, Johnny."

"Okay," Johnny said in a low voice. "I'll go on into town alone."

"Good luck." A terrible smile stretched Ken's pale lips for a moment. "Or maybe it's good-by."

"I'll be back, Ken."

Ken's raised face was haggard from the tension of the past hours. "I hope so, Johnny," he said tiredly.

Johnny went outside, moving onto the main road.

The town was three miles straight ahead. It was not much by any standards, just a tiny civic building, a restaurant, a pizza stand, a bar, a general store, a gas station, a few scattered houses. Two miles beyond town the forestry service had a large building and then there were a few more ranches. Once almost five hundred people had lived in Cinder Creek, now only about fifty. Once there had been a two-story hotel, another gas station, even a motel. But even before Johnny was born, the town had begun to die. But not like this, not all at once. . . .

It was six in the morning, and the sun was high and bright. Yesterday at this time Johnny had been helping his father feed the stock. They had talked about Johnny's older brother, Chuck, who would graduate with honors from college in Albuquerque. Chuck would come home then, and they were planning for the whole family to backpack into the mountains during the summer. Johnny's father was looking forward to that. Johnny wondered, sadly, what his father was thinking about now. He was a big rawboned man, frightened of very few things in the world. But now, perhaps he was scared. . . .

Danielle Frazer climbed dazedly through the dry brush of Cherimoya Canyon. She turned once and looked back, but she couldn't see the school any more.

Her legs were badly scratched from the dry chaparral, and one knee was bleeding from a nasty fall. "Johnny! Ken!" she shouted. Only the muted whisper of the wind stirring the brush replied.

Danielle shaded her eyes from the now brilliant sun and looked around, hoping she was going in the direction that the boys had gone. She moved on then, her legs numb, her breath coming in painful gasps.

Once she stopped and closed her eyes, and when she did she saw her father's face. She screamed at the image. "See what you've done? I hope you're satisfied, you and Mom—I hope you're satisfied!"

The sad-faced vision hung its head. "I'm sorry, baby. We tried, your mom and I. I don't know whose fault it was. She was always wanting, your mom was. Wanting, wanting. I felt like a dry well that somebody had come to too often—and still she wanted. Even when there was nothing left, she wanted. . . ."

When Danielle opened her eyes, he was gone. But she heard a strange, disembodied voice screaming, "Daddy, Daddy—oh please come and get me!" She did not recognize the voice as her own. She stumbled on, climbing the sloping, broken wall of the canyon. Something within her told her that she was going to die unless she kept moving, but suddenly she slowed, then stopped. She was simply too tired to go on. It didn't matter what happened.

72

"Hi," a male voice said.

At first Danielle thought it was a trick of the wind. Then she heard it again. "Hi. Are you lost?"

Danielle looked up and saw a young man about twenty years old with long, curly yellow hair. Shirtless, he was wearing jeans and cowboy boots. He was clean-shaven, with a broad, handsome face that reflected constant living under the sun.

"Oh thank God!" Danielle gasped. "I thought I'd never see another human being again!"

"My name is Alex. I'm hiking through the country. What are you doing wandering around a rough place like this?"

"I'm Danielle Frazer. I go to school at Cinder Creek High with twelve other kids . . . and oh, it's such a long, awful story I don't know where to begin."

"Tell you what, I've got a camper parked on the fire road. Come on up there with me and have a cold drink. Maybe you'll feel more like talking then."

Danielle nodded gratefully and took his offered hand, letting him lead her to an old camper van. He took her inside and she sat down at a dinette. He poured two cups of ginger ale and handed Danielle one. She gulped the sweet, fizzy liquid eagerly.

"Now, you were saying?" he asked.

"We can't waste time. See, all the kids in our school are being held prisoner. We don't even know what's happening. I mean, all kinds of weird things—the electricity is out, the phone, and they burned the Cinder Creek bridge, and they sent the school bus with nobody driving it and it crashed. . . ." She paused, seeing a smile playing around the boy's lips. "You don't believe me," she accused him.

"Well . . ."

"Oh *please* believe me. You must have seen the fire last night if you were around here. When the bridge burned, it lit up the whole sky."

He shook his head. "I've been around here for days and I didn't see any fire."

"Listen, just drive to a phone and call the sheriff—can you just do that?" His face blurred in front of her tired eyes until his skin seemed to become part of the cabinetry of the camper. A quizzical smile continued to linger around his lips. "I'll take care of it."

"You've got to help us," Danielle whispered, feeling the interior of the camper begin to revolve slowly like a carousel. She was so tired, so confused.

"I'll help you, of course. But first you must rest." He led Danielle to the bunk in the camper. Her legs felt like sticks of wet spaghetti. The inside of the vehicle was revolving rapidly now, almost like wash in the circular window of the family washing machine at home. As soon as she came in contact with the bed, she fell into an exhausted kind of sleep. Her limbs felt heavy and her eyes, even when open, seemed to be seeing a dream.

She saw the young man go to the stove and make himself coffee. He sat down at the small dinette and drank it slowly, almost in slow motion. From time to time he looked at her and she wondered if he believed her. He was obviously a wandering youth, just drifting, and perhaps he thought he'd found a companion, and that pleased him. Danielle wanted to scream at him, to make him believe her, but she didn't have the strength to do anything.

"Are you feeling better?" he asked her much later.

"You haven't gone for help yet, have you?"

"Yes. Yes, I have. When you were asleep. I went to a fire phone and called the sheriff. Everything is going to be okay." He smiled, and she noticed a copper medallion hanging around his neck, blending with his skin. It bore the likeness of a young man's head, something like a Roman bust. He noticed her staring at the medallion and he smiled again. "Do you like it? I had it made for myself last year in Taos. The man on the medal, he's sort of my namesake. Alexander the Great. I showed the man this picture I had of an old Macedonian coin and he copied it exactly."

"I feel so strange. So tired," Danielle said. "Was that really just ginger ale you gave me?"

"That was the elixir of life," he said. He came over

75

to the bunk and Danielle heard a clicking sound like a radio being turned on. "Ohhh . . . I feel so weird," she said.

In Room 1 at the school, Gayle and Sandra and Red McGinnis heard Danielle's voice. Gayle gasped, "That's Dany—her voice is coming over the PA system!" The others hurried into the room.

Everyone stared at the speaker as Danielle said, "It's like my arms and legs weigh a ton . . . ohhh, I feel awful. . . ."

Margaret's face showed anger, and her brown eyes shot up to the speaker. "If we can hear them, they can hear us. All right, whoever you are out there, why don't you stop playing your cowardly little games?"

Charlie stared at the speaker. "It's wild—they want to drive us all crazy."

There was a muffled laugh from the speaker, a man's voice, but nothing distinguishable. It lasted for about a minute, rising and falling, then there was silence.

"They're obviously mad," Margaret said bitterly.

"Come on outside, everybody," Valerie said. "We've got to talk without being overheard."

They gathered a few hundred yards from the school and Valerie told them, "Johnny and Ken didn't head for Carson Corners last night. They said that just to throw off whoever might be listening. They started for

76

Cinder Creek and they planned to cross over in a little boat Johnny knew of."

Bennie glanced at his watch. "If they got across okay they must have reached town hours ago. You know what that means, don't you?"

Hugh nodded grimly. "Yeah. They haven't found help yet. If they had then there'd be helicopters overhead and the place would be crawling with cops."

"They didn't make it," Red said in a tone of finality.

A look of anguish streaked through Valerie's eyes but she said nothing. Margaret spoke up quickly. "We don't know that."

"No," Hugh said, "but we can't just sit here expecting somebody is going to come in here and rescue us. We've got to make our own plans."

"Let's give Johnny and Ken till noon," Bennie suggested. "If nothing has happened by then, we'll make plans—and we keep quiet in the school so we don't tip anybody off." The others nodded in agreement.

At seven-fifteen, Johnny reached the gas station at the edge of town. He quickened his steps, a new impetus coming to his tired body. He couldn't see any signs of life, but there were cars as usual in the gas station, parked in the repair area. As he drew closer, he saw a large tiger cat jump off an old oil barrel and run around to the back of the station. It was somehow a reassuring sign. He had come to half believe Ken's awful suspicion that the world had come to some strange end.

When Johnny entered the gas station building, he found it empty. He went to the station pickup truck and looked in the cab. As he did, an unfamiliar voice said, "Is that your truck?"

Johnny turned slowly, seeing a young man in close-fitting black jeans with an animal-skin vest over his otherwise naked chest. His hair was black, close cropped, and he wore a copper medallion around his neck. "No, it's not mine," Johnny said slowly. He forced his voice to be cool in spite of a racing heart. "I was looking for Hal, the guy who runs the gas station." As Johnny spoke, he glanced anxiously around for something among Hal's tools which could serve as a weapon. He had his own pocketknife, but that wouldn't be very effective. He spied a pipe wrench a few feet away and decided he would try to get it at an opportune moment.

"Hal left me in charge." The young man moved closer.

"Where is everybody?" Johnny asked softly. "I mean, the town looks pretty empty."

"Yes. I guess everybody is down at the forestry building. The town was evacuated yesterday morning. Electricity went out. Phone, too. There were a few fires and some animals died." He was constantly moving closer to Johnny, a strangely desperate look in his eyes. Johnny decided he must make his move quickly. He whirled around and headed for the pipe wrench, but the man's voice stopped him short. "I have a gun."

Johnny stopped and turned around again. "Who are you?"

"Attila. Of course that's an adopted name. I've buried my given name. All significant men of history have adopted more appropriate names. Vladimir Illich became Lenin. Octavianus became Augustus. I became Attila."

Another youth in skintight dark jeans and an animal-skin vest appeared. He wore a headdress as well, a fur cap from which protruded two curled horns, one on each side of his head. He carried a deadly looking rifle, and a copper medallion glowed from his chest. An unnatural smile distorted his lips as he leveled the rifle at Johnny and asked his companion, "Can I shoot him now, Attila?"

8. Hide or Surrender?

"This," said Attila to Johnny, "is Eric the Red. You must forgive him. He's anxious to use his new rifle."

Johnny stared at the boy's face. "You're David Cole. You were in high school three or four years ago right here in town."

"I'm Eric the Red," he snapped.

A picture of a gaunt, red-haired youth of seventeen screaming hysterically at Mr. Farnsworth several years ago came sharply into Johnny's mind. He had been a senior, six months from graduation, and they had found "speed" in his locker. The penalty was swift and permanent. He was expelled. The disgrace was overwhelming in the tiny community, compelling the Coles to sell their ranch hastily and flee. Rumors of the family's continuing misfortune drifted back to Cinder Creek from time to time. David's parents had separated, and the boy had wandered into a San Francisco commune.

"Do you think this town owes you something or what, David?" Johnny asked.

"You call me that once more and I'll——" He aimed the rifle menacingly again. But Johnny noticed at that moment that the sun was in both their eyes, and he decided to try to make a break for it, perhaps dash around the back of the gas station and head for the thick brush. He had to get away from them if he was going to do himself or anybody else any good. He spun around and began his desperate run, but a hard object came crashing down on his head and the street came up, slamming him in the face. In the next moment, the earth floated away from his reach.

Johnny woke up in the civic building, tied to a swivel chair. His arms were pulled uncomfortably behind the chair and tough, coarse ropes bound his wrists and ankles. His head ached, sharing the fate of every other bone in his body. When he opened his eyes, he saw a very beautiful girl perched on top of the desk, her long, brown hair decorated with plastic flowers. "I'm Theodora," she said with a vacant smile, "but you may call me Dora. Theodora was Justinian's wife, you know. Justinian, he was some great leader from somewhere, but Theodora was the big brain,

81

and a real groovy chick too. Worked in a circus and trained bears and stuff. Hey, what's your name?"

Johnny shook his head, trying to clear the fuzziness. "Johnny Harrison. Can you tell me what's going on?"

Theodora looked across the room at Attila. "Can we tell him, Attila?"

"Tell him what?"

"What we're doing." She smiled at Johnny. "You're cute."

Attila got up and came over. Johnny could read the words on his medallion: *Scourge of God.* The girl also wore a medallion. Hers bore the profile of a beautiful Byzantine woman, probably somebody's concept of what Theodora looked like. "You want to know what we're doing? Sure. We're the new barbarians, and we're taking over the world—just like mushy, materialistic, overcivilized Rome was taken over by the old barbarians."

"You—a handful of people? You are taking over the world?"

Attila smiled. "Not just us. There's millions more like us. Most of them don't know it yet, and they're still hanging around communes and rock concerts, aimless. Just wait till we get it all together. We're just a small part, but we're one of the first. Four guys and a bird. Eric the Red put us onto this town, figured it would be as good a place as any to start. So we took it, easy as picking apples. Night before last we took the school. I killed the lights, the phones . . . easy. Then we went from house to house, told the old types we were from the repair crew. Then we told them we had their kids. It was so easy. They were so scared."

Dora giggled. "Eric had the idea about the school bus. Wasn't that great? I'll bet you were out of your minds when that happened."

"Where are the people from this town?" Johnny asked.

"Out in the old forestry building. 'We have met the enemy and they are ours.'"

"Who's the enemy?"

"Them. You know, the old ones. The relics. It's them against us. It's always been that way. The old ones have always ruled, holding the kids in bondage, forcing us to do their thing, play by their rules, even die for them. You ever think of that, Johnny? You ever think about who dies in the wars? You take the Civil War—half a million guys between fifteen and twenty-four died. Why? Did guys that age own plantations or own big northern factories? No, man. The old guys made the money, the young guys died. It's the same now. The pollution thing. Who owns the factories dumping tons of poison in the air, the rivers? It's the old types who figure to be gone when the world turns around and bites back."

"Okay, so maybe you got a point. But what you're doing here is crazy. You can't get away with it."

"That isn't nice," Dora said petulantly. She came over to Johnny and ran her fingers through his thick black hair. "Attila said we already got away with it."

Attila gave Johnny's chair a violent spin, turning him around in dizzying circles. "That's right, we've already done it. We got maybe twenty thousand dollars, some jewelry, guns. We took the town. We've got the people on their knees. Hey, Johnny, how about you joining us? You seem like a tough, courageous guy. You part Indian? From your skin color and cheekbones, I'd say you are. You could be Geronimo, that fabulous guy from your heritage. We'll get you a medallion with his picture on it and you can be part of the future."

"I wouldn't disgrace Geronimo's memory," Johnny snapped. In response, Attila gave the swivel chair another spin, kicking it into motion with the pointed toe of his cowboy boot. Nausea swept Johnny. Attila produced the knife he'd removed from Johnny's pocket and snapped the blade out a few inches from Johnny's throat. "You can be part of *our* future or *their* past. You understand, man?"

Johnny stared at the young man. "Did you hurt anybody when you took over?" He was thinking of his father now. Johnny's mother had been dead for many years. Since Chuck had gone to college, it was just the two of them, Johnny and his dad.

Attila shrugged. "Who knows? I don't remember erasing any of the old types myself."

"My dad," Johnny said, emotion crowding into his voice, "he's a big dark guy . . . maybe you remember him——"

Attila stared at Johnny, "You that concerned about your old man, Johnny boy?"

"Yeah."

"You hear that, Dora? You ever hear something so far out? The hero here likes his old man. He must be some super kind of old type to rate that. Now you take *my* old man!" He laughed in an ugly way. "But that's another story."

He turned back to Johnny. "Listen, man, you just think about joining us. You think real hard." He gave the swivel chair a passing kick and left the room with Theodora.

When they were gone, Johnny strained violently at the ropes, but it was a waste of time. He gave an exhausted sigh and wondered if whether Ken would be able to do any good. A prayer formed in his mind— a prayer that Ken would somehow find a way to do something that would help.

Danielle watched the blond young man moving around the camper, but she was still not sure she wasn't dreaming. There were garish pictures on the camper's walls, revolutionary posters of clenched fists, and *youth power* scrawled in red paint. "Alex," she said, and he turned. "Alex, who are you?"

"Just Alex. My friends call me Alexander the Great after that guy who conquered most of the world before he was thirty. I like Alex better than the stupid name I was stuck with by the old types. We are all known by special names."

"Who are *we*?"

"Oh, me and my friends."

"You're one of them, aren't you?" she said, at last knowing the truth. "You are one of those people who've been doing those awful things to us."

The pleasant look left his face. "We had to."

"Why did you have to?"

"Like Attila says—he's our leader—we need money. We got a lot of money in the town, and we proved we could do something like this. That's important because we're going to knock over the whole stinking society, piece by piece. Everybody is afraid of us. That's the big weapon. Attila says people will fight what they know, but if you make it so they don't know what they're fighting, then they go crazy with panic and it's easy to take them when the time comes. The old types are afraid of kids anyway. Not just us, but all the kids. You read it in the magazines and newspapers—they're hostile and afraid because they know we're taking over from them and their time is almost up."

Danielle shook her head in confusion. "It's all so strange—sometimes I think I'm crazy or something and this isn't really happening. My father had me to a shrink a couple of times, you know. Maybe I'm crazy and that's why none of it figures. . . ."

He reached over suddenly and covered her hand with his. She thought how warm his hand was. Nobody had ever done that with her before. She felt good about it—confused, but good. Sometimes she wanted her parents to hug her like some parents hugged their kids. She'd even seen big old Charlie Harrison hug six-foot-tall Johnny as if he was a little kid. But Danielle's mother was distant and her father even more so. Once Danielle was so frightened she'd wanted to hide herself in her father's arms, but he had dropped his arms and said, "No, Danielle, you're much too old for this sort of thing."

Alex asked, "Who do you like from history, Danielle?"

"I don't know. I've wanted to be brave, but I'm always scared. I wanted to be strong enough to take whatever happened and never, ever be scared. I read about a French girl once who led a whole army and then got burned at the stake and she must have been pretty brave to do that."

"Joan of Arc," he said. "Okay, you are forthwith Joan of Arc. We'll get you a silver medallion with a lily banner on it." His smile widened and he put his arm around Danielle. "Would you like that?" She didn't say anything, but she didn't push him away, either.

It was ten o'clock and Danielle's voice came over the loudspeaker. Everybody gathered to listen. She spoke slowly, mechanically, as if she were reading from a paper. "The people of Cinder Creek are prisoners. Johnny Harrison is also a prisoner, so he cannot help you. Nobody can help you. You must go outside and wait at the flagpole, and when the camper van comes you will surrender. If you don't do this, then Johnny Harrison will be shot first and then the others." She signed off abruptly.

Valerie gasped, "Oh—they have Johnny!"

Bennie motioned for everybody to go outside, out of hearing distance. When this was done, he said, "They didn't mention Ken. Perhaps Ken got through."

"What have they done to her?" Gayle wept. "She sounds like a stranger!"

"She was obviously forced to read their note," Margaret said. "The point is, we've got to decide what to do."

"Surrendering to them would be stupid," Red said quickly. "We don't even know if anybody in town is still alive. We don't even know what or who they are. I mean . . . they could be murderous maniacs. . . ."

"I certainly won't just go there like they ask," Suzanne said, "and I think anybody who does is crazy.

God only knows what they plan to do to us. I think we ought to get out of here right now. Just head for the nearest, heaviest brush. I don't care where—just as far as we can get."

Hugh glanced at his sister. Tears were standing in her eyes, and he could tell she'd already made her decision. He slipped his arm around her shoulders. "You want to do what they say, don't you?"

"Oh Hugh, Mom and Dad . . ."

"Yeah," he said huskily, "I feel like that too."

Suzanne shrugged. "We have to think of ourselves. I'm sorry if that sounds selfish, but I've only known my grandparents for a short time and they're . . . old. I mean, we have our whole lives ahead of us. I'm certainly not going to die for them—or for anybody."

Janet always followed Suzanne's lead. She found it hard to do this time, but she managed. "I don't think my parents would want me to give myself over to those awful people."

Suzanne said in a businesslike tone, "I'm leaving right now. I don't think there's any time to lose. Who's coming?"

Margaret looked at Bennie. "I can't help it—I can't be rational now. My folks . . . and Johnny . . ."

Bennie nodded. "Yeah."

Valerie's decision had been made the moment the threat was issued. There would be no sense in living if everyone she loved were dead. Gayle was too frightened to make a break with the others, so Suzanne's group finally included Janet, Red and Charlie. As Suzanne left, she looked at Valerie apologetically. "Hey, I'm sorry, Val. But it's the old survival thing, you know." Valerie nodded, saying nothing.

The six who remained behind went out to the flagpole and waited. A strong, warm wind was blowing and Valerie's long pale hair tangled on her back. She looked up and realized that there was no flag on the pole. They always raised it during the morning pledge, and Mr. Farnsworth led the ceremony. With a deep shudder, Valerie wondered where they all were, all the familiar, ordinary people she'd always taken for granted.

The van came in twenty minutes. It rolled quickly into view, enveloped in its own dust. It was ordinary-looking, but old. The young man at the wheel got out, a rifle in his arms. He was thin, vaguely homely, not striking in any way. He wore no shirt, but a medallion glowed on his chest bearing the likeness of the nineteenth-century Italian revolutionary Garibaldi. His eyes were dull.

His companion wore a fur cap with curled horns, and his rifle was aimed directly at the six. He displayed an eagerness to use it. He stepped forward. "Where are the others? There were thirteen. We have two, so five are missing."

"They decided to leave," Margaret said curtly. "Who

are you?" she demanded. "Are you all crazy or did you take too many little colored pills?"

Garibaldi grinned suddenly. "Hey, she's a spunky one."

Margaret continued to look at Eric, recognizing him then. "Say, you used to go to school here."

"I'm Eric the Red. Nobody else," he said. "Garibaldi, check the school and see if anybody's in there."

Valerie exchanged a look with Margaret, both of them recalling the sad kid and his unhappy family. They hadn't been in high school at the time, but most of the kids who were, ignored the boy at their parents' demand. Chuck Harrison had been the one exception. Johnny's older brother had even gone so far as to plead with Mr. Farnsworth to reconsider the expulsion, but the elderly principal was terrified that the problem would spread. Although he was really a kind man, he considered David Cole victim of a deadly disease, which must be isolated and exterminated for the sake of the others.

Garibaldi came out of the school. "Empty in there."

Eric leveled his rifle. "Where did they go?"

"I haven't the slightest idea," Margaret said.

Eric aimed his rifle at a sapling and shattered it with a burst of fire. "You sure you don't know?"

Hugh decided they wouldn't settle for no information, so he came up with some false directions. "I saw them. They headed for Armadillo Canyon, north."

Eric's cold eyes swept the group. "We better find them there or you're all done for." He went to the van and used the radio to advise somebody in town. He brought handcuffs and manacled the boys' hands behind their backs before herding them into the van. Then he ordered the girls in.

"Where are we going?" Valerie asked, staring around the inside of the van at garish posters.

"You'll see," Eric snapped.

"Is Johnny all right?"

He looked away from the wheel. "You in love with him?"

"I care very much for him. . . ."

"Bet a little blond bird like you wouldn't give a guy like me a second look," Eric said.

"Please, is he all right?"

"Last I heard he was," Eric said in a bored voice.

"Where are our families?" Margaret said.

"Locked up for now. Who cares about the old types, anyway?"

"We all do," Margaret said angrily. "Why don't you tell us what you want?"

"Power, baby!" Eric laughed. "Everything. The world."

Garibaldi said, "You know that the first Garibaldi . . . he took over Italy with a thousand kids in red shirts. Attila says we can take over the world." He looked at Sandra. "How about you, little brown girl. You got a guy?"

Sandra's dark eyes flashed, but she said nothing.

"Aw . . ." Garibaldi grinned. "Is that black guy yours?"

"She's my sister," Hugh snarled. "Leave her alone."

Garibaldi's grin widened. "You can't do nothing, guy. I could take her if I wanted and you couldn't do nothin'."

"I'll kick your brains in," Hugh said coldly.

Garibaldi turned to Margaret. "You want to take off them glasses and let me see what you look like?"

"I happen to need them," Margaret told him disgustedly.

Garibaldi reached back, snatching them from her face. "Hey, you're kinda cute."

"Give those back to me!" Margaret stormed. "You give those back to me!"

Garibaldi laughed gleefully and stuffed the glasses in his belt. "You be nice, little girl, or I'll bust them for you."

The van jolted to a stop at an old stone house. Eric said, "Everybody out." Valerie recognized the place as having once belonged to David Cole's family. It was where they had been living when the boy was expelled from school. Ever since that time it had stood abandoned. The windows were long since broken. Some ghost stories about the place had circulated in town and most people stayed away from the house.

The six teen-agers were ordered down a narrow stairway into the basement. Gayle moaned in fear at entering the damp, musty cellar. Scratching sounds in the corners of the room made pictures of rats rise in her mind. Garibaldi unlocked the cuffs of the boys. He purposely dropped Margaret's glasses at her feet, but they didn't break.

"Don't try to get out," Eric advised. "The air vents aren't big enough and there's only one door—and that's going to be locked. If anybody fools with that door, then don't be surprised if rifle fire goes off in your face."

"How long do you expect to keep us here?" Bennie asked.

"Until we decide what to do," Eric told him. With that he went back up the stairs, opening and closing the door, and they could hear the heavy sound of a bolt going into place.

It was Bennie who spoke first. "I hate to think of what they'll do to us eventually if we don't find a way out."

"Maybe," Sandra said with more hope than confidence, "Ken got through to the next town. . . ."

9. The Death of Janet?

Ken Tillich made himself a sandwich and moved around the family home, going into each room to convince himself that everyone was truly gone. He stared at his parents' room—neat, beautiful—at his brothers' rooms—at Tommie's riding trophies, Harry's airplane models. Nothing seemed disturbed except that the matching pistols, which had been mounted on the wall in the den, were missing.

It was noon when Ken heard a sound at the door. He froze in panic. They had come for him, whoever they were. He looked frantically around for some possible weapon, and his gaze settled on the fireplace where an iron poker lay. He grabbed it and went slowly to the door. Before he opened it, he peered cautiously through the curtain.

His fear changed to joy. "Why, it's Queenie!" he

cried, seeing his collie scratching patiently to be let in. He swung the door open and the dog jumped up, licking his face. "Hey, girl! Wow, am I glad to see you! I wish you could talk and tell me what's happening."

Ken let the dog in and closed the door, but the action had been costly. A camper truck appeared suddenly in the street as if out of nowhere. When Ken closed the door, the truck stopped. Hurriedly, he put the chain across the door. He looked at his dog, whose intelligent eyes regarded him from a tilted head, almost as if she were pleading that he do something.

A youth with a strange horned headdress shouted from the truck, "Come out of that house." Ken stared in horror through the curtain as the young man pointed a rifle through the van window. "We have taken everyone at the school and in the town prisoner. You have no chance."

Ken's mind fumbled to understand. How could they have come from the school when the bridge was gone? Then he remembered the fire road winding through the back country. It was a good fifteen miles long, but someone who knew it was there could cut through.

Ken's body was instantly washed in perspiration. He hit the floor as a volley of gunfire ripped through the front door and sent a shower of wood splinters across the shag rug.

"Come out!" the stranger called. "The next time I fire, it won't be high enough to miss you!"

Ken crawled across the floor of the living room and into the kitchen. He peered out the back door and saw no one there. "Queenie, you stay," he whispered, crouching and easing his body out the back door. Behind the house stood the empty corrals and then open brush country. If he could make it to the outcroppings of rock, he'd have some chance.

Ken ran through the corrals, vaulting over one fence. He was about a hundred yards from the rocks when the van rolled around the back of the house and cut him off.

Ken watched, terror stricken, as the van seemed to be coming right for him. But suddenly a profound change came over him. Suddenly he knew he could not run this time, he *would* not run this time. He stood where he was, on the sandy earth, staring at the swelling grillwork of the van, watching almost with detachment as it hurtled toward him. He felt the sand pellets from the wheels sting his face, but still he did not move. He was prepared to die and a kind of peace touched him. And then he realized that the van had gone by, its fender brushing his trousers. But he was still standing.

Eric stepped out first, his rifle in his hand. "Where are the others?" he demanded. When Ken didn't answer him, Eric came at him in a rage, cracking him

97

over the head with the rifle stock. A billion lights exploded before Ken's eyes. He didn't even see the earth come up and fill his mouth with sand.

They opened the cellar door again and half shoved, half dragged Ken down the stairs. Eric's eyes smoked with anger as he leveled the rifle. "We found him in town, not in any canyon. The truth now."

Valerie spoke up quickly, sensing how dangerous the man was. "Johnny and Ken came into town together. The others left from the school. We really don't know where they went."

Ken lay crumpled at the bottom of the stairs, dazed. Eric pointed the rifle directly at him, but looked at Valerie. "I always hated games, even as a little kid. Now I'm going to——"

"You can't," Margaret said. "That would be murder."

"No," he corrected her. "War. War, honey. Civil war. The revolution, them against us. Military necessity." But he lowered the rifle. "You better hope we find the others." He went back up the stairs and locked the door again.

In the civic office in town, Theodora let herself into the room where Johnny was. "No luck with the ropes, Geronimo?" Johnny merely looked at her, too miserable for speech.

98

Attila came into the room then. "We got your friend Ken in case you had some hopes in that direction."

"Hey, man." Theodora looked at Johnny. "You want a drink?" He said nothing, but she went outside and got him an orange drink from the machine. She held it to his lips. When he had finished it, he thanked her.

Attila suddenly cut Johnny's ropes, and for the first few seconds Johnny almost fainted with the pain of blood rushing back into his limbs. Everything turned black, then slowly cleared. When he could see again, there was a pistol in Attila's hand. "Right now my friends are taking a last look through some of the stores and houses for anything valuable. Around dusk we're leaving—with recruits or maybe with hostages."

"You'd better not harm anybody if you don't want real trouble."

"Easy, man," Attila said. "This is a revolution. Like some old type said once, what revolution was ever made without bloodshed? Don't you warn me, Johnny boy. Who cares about harming people in a revolution or in a war?" A slow fury came into his dark eyes. "You take war, for instance. Anybody say 'don't drop the bomb there—might be kids playing'? Not on your life, man. My old man was a bombardier in the 'big war,' as he calls it. He never stopped bragging. And when my older brother got the right age, he wanted to cop out of it, but my old man says 'I done my duty, and no son of mine is going to do less. . . .' So my brother goes and in a few months he's coming home in a long narrow box and my old man is nothing but proud.

"Why don't he even cry, I wonder . . . and then they pull my number and he expects me to make him proud too. Like the Aztecs used to cut out the hearts from young guys in every generation so the old types would have a good crop or something. I told my old man I wasn't going, and he smacks me in the mouth and calls me a coward. So then I smacked him back—busted his jaw—and I got out of there. If I'm going to die in a war, it's going to mean something. It's going to be *my* war."

Theodora said with feeling, "My parents were skunks, too."

Attila laughed. "You didn't have any parents, Dora."

She looked hurt. "I did too. Just because I never knew them doesn't mean I never had any. Everybody has got to have parents."

"They put her in the trash can when she was born," Attila explained to Johnny.

Theodora hung her head until her brown hair almost covered her face. "You didn't have to go and tell him that, Attila."

"Not everybody's parents are like that," Johnny said. "You get good and bad in all generations. You can't put down a whole generation just because they've lived longer than you."

Attila shrugged. "All I'm saying is we're going to rule for a change. No more busting kids for crimes the old types get away with. No more getting nailed for grass when they get stoned on booze. No more schools that are like jails. No more wars with kids getting their heads shaved like for execution."

"You can't build your world the way you want it—not like this," Johnny said.

"We got to, man. There ain't no turning back," said Attila.

In one of the tangled canyons, progress was slow for the four who moved through the brush. "Can't you go any faster, Charlie?" Suzanne demanded. You're holding us all back."

Charlie grimaced from his sore feet. "I'm no hiker. I'm doing the best I can."

"How many more miles do you think before we reach help?" Janet asked.

Suzanne shrugged. "How should I know? Maybe Charlie or Red could trap us something to eat. I'm almost fainting with hunger."

"My old man took me rabbit hunting a coupla times, but we had guns," Charlie said. "How can we get anything without guns?"

"Maybe we'll find a stream with fish in it," Red said longingly. "Or some berries."

"Man, my feet are on fire," Charlie complained. "How long we been walking now?"

Suzanne looked at her watch. It had been a gift from her parents on her sixteenth birthday. "About two, two and a half hours."

"When are we going to rest?" Charlie demanded.

"Oh Charlie, don't be totally stupid!" Suzanne snapped. "You know they're looking for us, and they probably know these canyons better than we do."

"We'll make it, won't we, Suzy?" Janet asked.

"Oh," Suzanne said crossly, "don't you start whining now! I'm not the tooth fairy or Santa Claus!"

Red stubbed his toe on a rock and let out a yell.

"Don't be such a crybaby!" Suzanne told him. "Sometimes I think Margaret is right about men being as weak as women!"

"Margaret's a stupid fool," Charlie said. "Otherwise why did she and the others turn themselves over to those guys?"

Janet frowned a little. "She did it for her family and for Johnny. That's why they all did it."

"Big deal." Charlie scoffed. "Six kids committing suicide."

"Oh, don't say that, Charlie!" Janet cried.

"If you think it was so great to stay behind, then why didn't you do it?" Red demanded.

Janet flushed. "I didn't have the courage.

"Oh, Suzy!" Janet's face twisted with anguish. "You

don't think they're going to kill everybody, do you?" The thought of her parents and her friends being dead struck her with sudden force. She didn't understand her parents very well, and they didn't seem to understand her at all, but she really did love them. She began to weep softly.

"Stop sniffling!" Suzanne cried irritably. "That's all we need—Oh Jan, don't be an idiot!"

"But Suzy—our folks, our friends———" Janet suddenly felt all alone in the world.

"Sniveling isn't going to change anything!"

"It's not as bad for you," Janet said defensively. "Your parents are safe somewhere."

"I never had any parents." Suzanne's voice was bitter. "I just had two people who put me in boarding school the minute one would accept me. I learned very early in life that everybody has just one person they can depend on—themselves. It's time you learned that too, Janet."

Red thought about his father, sitting at the kitchen table with the ever-present can of beer open before him; always the can of beer. But it had been different once. When Red was small and his mother was still alive, Red's father had taken him fishing and to the zoo even, one summer. He was fun in those days, before his business failed, before his wife died. Red swallowed hard and wished he could see his father again, if only just to tell him that he remembered those good times too, that he knew he hadn't always been a sad shadow sitting in front of an empty can of beer. "We don't know for sure that everybody's dead," Red declared.

"It don't help thinking about it anyway," Charlie said. "I guess my old man made out if anybody did. I think he'd probably make a deal with the devil to get home free."

"Like us, huh Charlie?" Janet said.

Charlie flushed. "What do you want to say a thing like that for?"

"Quit bickering!" Suzanne said. "We've got to save all our energy for walking." Her voice broke off. Then, "I hear a car—or a truck or something!"

"Yeah, I smell exhaust," Red cried. "Hey, I bet it's one of *them* after us!"

"Quick, let's get into heavy brush and hide until they've gone," Suzanne said. They began to run toward thicker undergrowth. As they did, Janet let out a short cry of pain as her ankle twisted on a rock. She tried to scramble away from the suddenly slipping earth, but a small slide was triggered by her kicking the rock. She lost her footing on the sloping side of the canyon and began to slip down into a ravine.

"Janet!" Suzanne shouted, watching the other girl rolling and tumbling until she was lying at the bottom of a twenty-foot gully. She rushed over to the edge. "Janet, are you okay?"

Janet raised a pale, frightened face. "My leg. I can't move it——"

"You think it's busted?" Charlie asked.

"I don't know," she sobbed.

"That car is coming closer." Red started away from the ravine.

"Does anybody have a rope or anything to pull her out?" Suzanne looked at the boys.

"There isn't *time*——" Red blurted.

Suzanne peered over the edge. "Janet, listen. Be very quiet and maybe they won't see you. We've got to take cover and then we'll be back to help you."

Tears streamed down Janet's face. "Oh, please, don't leave me all alone!"

"We have to," Suzanne shouted over her shoulder as she and the boys ran into the brush.

In another few minutes they saw a van truck bouncing across the rocky country. It stopped a few hundred yards away and two men stepped out. From their hidden position, the three could barely see the men, only that they wore no shirts and that one had a strange horned headdress.

"He looks like a monster." Charlie shuddered.

"Shhh," Suzanne cautioned.

The strange-looking men carried rifles, and the sun blazed on the medallions they wore around their necks. They were moving in the direction where Janet was. Suzanne bit her lip and looked away quickly. It wasn't her fault Janet had fallen, she told herself. She had no choice but to leave her. Why sacrifice more lives in a silly gesture? Still she winced when Charlie whispered, "I think they've seen her—they sound excited."

In a few minutes rifle fire filled the air. Charlie and Red turned white. Suzanne closed her eyes. They could not see what was happening because the van was between them and the ravine and it was some distance off.

"We shouldn't have left her." Red groaned in remorse.

"Shh—will you?" Suzanne whispered.

"Oh Lord," Charlie said, "why did they have to shoot her?" He was silent as the footsteps came again, the sound of the van doors opening and slamming. The three looked at each other in silent terror and desperately tried to crouch deeper into the brush.

10. The Three Escape

Somehow the two men did not see Suzanne and the boys, although they walked so close that the teen-agers heard their boots crunch. Eventually they turned around, went back to their van and drove off down the fire road.

"They're going!" Charlie gasped in disbelief.

"Let's get going ourselves while we still can." Suzanne got quickly to her feet and brushed the dust off her skirt.

Red spoke with difficulty. "Shouldn't we . . ."

"Shouldn't we what?" Suzanne's lower lip trembled. "Go over there and look at her? Just to torture our-selves with a feeling of guilt we don't deserve?"

"But maybe she isn't . . ." Red stammered.

"Of course she is. She must be." Suzanne noticed where the rifle fire had sheared off some small trees.

107

"Look, they even killed the trees. They're maniacs! Will you come on?"

Red continued to stand there, dazed. "I took her out once, just for pizza. She acted like it was a big deal. I wish I'd taken her out a few more times."

"For heaven's sake, Red, will you stop that?" Suzanne cried angrily.

"I never been close to anybody who died, never," Red mumbled. "Except Mom. And she was sick a long time. She was in the hospital a year before she died. It's funny, our class with just a few kids and one's dead already. Hey, Suzy, you know what she always said? She always said she wanted to be like you . . . just like you."

"You're acting as if *we* killed her." Suzanne's anger flared again. "Or *I* killed her. Well, it's not our fault— we didn't make her fall, and we didn't bring those awful monsters here."

"We just left her, like strangers would—like the worst kind of strangers." Red hated himself more than he ever had in his entire life.

"We did the best we could," Charlie said. And the three of them continued toward where they believed Carson Corners would eventually be.

At the old Cole place, the heavy door at the top of the stairs opened again. It was four-thirty in the afternoon. Attila and Eric moved down the stairs, armed as usual with rifles. "We're about to leave your crummy little community," Attila announced. "We got plenty of money and other things that will come in handy, and a lot of satisfaction. Only we need something else." He paused as Eric beamed a flashlight into the faces of the six prisoners. "Any volunteers for our cause?"

There was a deep silence. Ken, his head still aching, leaned against one wall. Gayle was sobbing steadily, and Sandra was trying to comfort her.

"Okay, hostages then," Attila said. "You, blondie." He pointed to Valerie. "And that sassy little bird with the braids, and the guy with the glasses."

Valerie, Margaret and Bennie came forward.

"Okay," Attila announced. "I'm locking the door again—when you eventually bust out, we'll be far enough away for it not to matter."

The three hostages were herded upstairs and out to the van. They drove to the civic building, stopping briefly. Attila unrolled a piece of butcher paper. "We got a big proclamation here. When the old types eventually get out of the forestry building, they're going to find this tacked to the civic-building door. It says: *To the past people of Cinder Creek. Thanks for the money and the hospitality. See you at the revolution.* And it's going to be signed by us—and by you." He paused, handing the paper, with a pen, to Margaret. "You first."

"Why that's ridiculous," Margaret protested. "I have nothing but contempt for your silly revolution."

Attila did not smile when he repeated his request. "How about I shoot your friend with the glasses?" He waved his rifle at Bennie. Margaret made a face and signed. Bennie and Valerie did the same. Then Attila went into the civic building where Theodora waited. He unlocked Johnny's handcuffs and pushed the paper at him. "We're leaving town with hostages, Geronimo. You're one of them. But first I want you to sign this paper."

Johnny stared at the crude document. "Our families won't believe we mean this."

"Sign," Attila said harshly, and Johnny complied. Attila ordered the boy outside and Johnny slowly walked toward the van. When Valerie saw him, she gasped in relief and he managed a quick smile in response. Valerie and Johnny were placed in one van, Margaret and Bennie in the other. The boys were handcuffed.

It was five in the afternoon as the two vans rolled from Cinder Creek, turning east. The butcher-paper proclamation was secured to the civic-building door with a long-bladed knife and it fluttered slightly in the afternoon breeze. The vans were quickly swallowed up in the dust and the haze of the foothills.

Johnny figured they were gradually moving toward the Mexican border and would attempt to cross at a

110

desolate place. He glanced into the front seat at Alex, who drove, and at Danielle, who sat very close to him, seeming to be utterly content with the situation. Danielle appeared to have crossed the thin, invisible line between the real and unreal world. Once she looked back at Valerie and Johnny and, smiling in a vague, offhand way as one does to an old friend not seen in a long time and half forgotten, seemed to find nothing amiss.

"They probably drugged her," Johnny whispered to Valerie. Valerie nodded, still so overwhelmed with relief that Johnny was all right that even her fears had temporarily vanished.

At dusk the two vans pulled into a cottonwood grove beside a secluded creek. Everyone got out. The sky was cooling and darkening, turning a deeper blue.

Johnny noticed Dany standing alone by the creek, and he approached her slowly, keeping his voice even. "How's it going, Dany?"

"Okay, Johnny." She smiled, though her eyes looked strange. "It's going to be all right now. I know it is." She glanced at the boy's handcuffs and looked momentarily unhappy, but the mood passed swiftly. "I've got a new name, Johnny. My name is Joan now and I'm not afraid like I used to be. Alexander is going to get me a nice medallion for around my neck. Isn't that neat?"

"Yes, I'm glad," Johnny said gently.

"Oh Johnny, you should hear Alex talk." The smile danced precariously on her lips. "He says such cool things. I understand everything he says, Johnny, because he talks so good. You remember back at school how I always got bad marks on my report cards? Well, it was between a D and an F most of the time in history, and now I know why that was. Those teachers talked so fast I never understood them. Do you remember how fast Mrs. Boswell used to talk, Johnny?" She laughed a high-pitched, nervous laugh. "I never could take notes good enough to pass, but Alexander explains things and makes them real easy."

"I see," Johnny said. He had hoped he could perhaps reach Danielle and get her to help him and the others escape. But now he doubted that she'd be of any help.

"Alex is really smart, Johnny. He says that the old people have wrecked everything with wars and stuff and we young people got a chance now to make it all right. Oh, he's so cool. He says we don't really need schools, anyway not the kind of schools that make you feel dumb all the time. And no more cops busting people for every little thing. Oh, and the best thing —*the very best thing*—Johnny, he says he loves me. He really said that, and I believe him. Nobody ever said that to me before, Johnny. Nobody. . . ." Her smile flitted away and her eyes narrowed in worry for a moment. "It's going to be all right, isn't it, Johnny?"

He nodded with a weak smile. He could not risk telling her otherwise. She was very close to the edge, and he didn't want to push her somewhere from which she might not come back.

In an outcropping of rock near the creek, Margaret braided her hair and wondered how they would get out of this nightmare. A shadow fell across her and she looked up to see Garibaldi. He shot up a nervous left hand and smoothed down his hair. In the other arm he cradled his rifle, almost tenderly. "You always carry that, don't you?" Margaret asked critically. "Like a security blanket."

"Huh?" He did not know what a security blanket was.

"Nothing." Margaret sighed.

"Which one is your guy?"

"I don't have a guy. I'm too busy with my own life."

He grinned. "How come you're not nicer to me then?"

Margaret decided to change the subject. "What are you doing in this stupid gang anyway?"

"It ain't so stupid. I stuck up some gas stations by myself and I used to get maybe twenty dollars. Now we got pretty near thirty thousand, Attila says." He paused, appearing in deep thought. "How much more than twenty dollars is thirty thousand? Ten times, a hundred times maybe?"

Margaret looked at him in surprise. "You mean you can't figure that?"

He looked immediately angry. "Don't you laugh at me!"

"I'm not," Margaret said quickly, and he relaxed a little.

"I just never bothered to learn that junk. I don't bother with reading neither. It just hurts your eyes. Anyway, they wouldn't let me in school when I was a kid. See, this old man who ran the school—the head guy . . ." His eyes began to gleam. "Like that Farnsworth. The principal. Yeah, well this old guy when I was a kid, he told my old man that I couldn't go to school with the other kids."

"Why not?" Margaret asked.

He shrugged his big shoulders. "I was ten or somewhere in there, maybe eleven. I was going to be in the—the second grade I think. Maybe third. I was a little bit bigger than the other kids. See, I was big for my age. . . ." A long-buried agony came into his narrow eyes. "The head guy, he asked me to read this book about some kids and a dog, but I couldn't read it. I tried to make a story up from the pictures, but the old guy says I'm retared . . . something like that. He says retared kids ain't wanted in regular school. Boy, was my old man sore. He says he never heard of such a thing. He says I shamed him, and he beat the daylights out of me 'cause he says it must be something

114

I done to be retared. . . . Hey, girl, you know what retared is? Is it a guy's fault if he's retared?"

"I believe the word is *retarded*," Margaret said, feeling suddenly sorry for the boy in spite of everything. "It isn't anybody's fault."

He smiled a little, pleased at that. "But, see, my old man, he blamed me. He said I musta done something. So he says I got to go back to that school and make that old man take me. But he wouldn't. He got real mad and said I better go home or he'd call somebody. But I didn't go home." He began to smile. "I hung around that school till night and then I got in and I busted everything and made a nice big fire. . . ." The smile died in pain. "But they got me then and put me in this place with crazy people. But I'm not crazy. I'm not . . . retar retar—*you know.*"

Margaret stood up. "I'm very sorry. It must have been terrible for you."

He grinned maliciously. "I got out of that place where they put me. And do you know what? When we came to that school of yours, I found one of them books about the kids and the dog and I tried to read from it. I made that old Farnsworth listen, and then I said he should make me out a grade. He wouldn't, but then I shook him real hard and he got all white and he made me a grade—he gave me an A grade. He says I'm real smart. I didn't read for him no better than I

115

read for that old man when I was a kid, but Farnsworth said I was real smart. . . ."

Margaret stared at him. "You didn't hurt Mr. Farnsworth, did you?"

"Not much. Hey, you want some cherry soda?"

"I don't think so."

"I'm gonna get some cherry soda, and you have to drink some too."

"All right," Margaret said, following him reluctantly into the camper. He poured two glasses with great ceremony. Margaret hoped it wasn't spiked with anything.

"Now we got to hit the glasses together like they do in the movies," Garibaldi said, touching the rim of his glass to Margaret's. When Margaret finished drinking the cherry soda and set the glass down, he reached for her suddenly and kissed her. Margaret was startled and she drew back.

Garibaldi smiled crookedly. "Girls don't like me unless I make them." His face clouded. "But that's okay. Attila says I can have all I want."

He stood there pondering that as Margaret turned and left the camper in silence. Her heart was pounding with a combination of fear and pity. When she saw Bennie, she ran toward him.

11. "Better Than Dying"

Johnny walked to the front of one of the campers. Attila was working on the engine. He wiped the grease off his hands and looked at Johnny.

"Anytime you want to join up with us, you can get rid of those handcuffs, Geronimo."

Johnny ignored the offer. "Where are we headed?" Attila was too sharp to be conned into accepting a phony recruitment.

"Mexico for a while. But we'll be back. There'll be other Cinder Creeks, a thousand of them. Then bigger towns, then cities."

"Attila, you got me puzzled. Garibaldi isn't bright, and Alex and Eric are high on some mind blower. But you're smart and you seem straight in the head. It doesn't figure that a guy like you would get into something like this."

Attila shrugged. "I was going to be an electrical engineer. That's how come it was so easy for me to rig up bugs and radios. I guess I should be a nice little college boy about now . . . except when they came for me on the draft-dodging bit, I shot my way out of an attic. I didn't kill anybody, but . . . well, Geronimo, do you know very much about prisons—what it's like in those places?" He grinned suddenly. "And then maybe I'm a little bit crazy too. Only crazy people make things happen, man. You think Hitler was sane? But he almost took over the entire world."

"You figure Hitler accomplished something worthwhile? Who do you want to build gas chambers for, Attila?"

"You talk very big for somebody wearing handcuffs, Geronimo. I wouldn't need a gas chamber to turn you off."

"But, in spite of everything, you find that hard to do—and that bothers you," Johnny said, sensing some weakness in the dark young man's armor, some reluctance to descend totally to savagery.

"You're begging for no more tomorrows, man." Attila's dark eyes narrowed. Then his mood changed. "Okay, so when I finally decide to finish you, you're going to have to give me a good reason. That makes me better than most of the old types, doesn't it? I mean, if I can't kill you as easy as they've been killing women and children for forty years with all those nice little bombs, then all those old types are lower than me, right? And you, Geronimo, when *and if* you get to be nineteen, how many women and children are you willing to kill if it comes to that?"

"We're working for peace, man," Johnny said softly.

"Yeah? How? You singing songs about brotherhood? You maybe carrying posters, even laying down in the street in front of government buildings? Big deal. Kid stuff. You think they care? You think they'll stop? No. What I'm doing is for real. I'm robbing them. I'm recruiting their kids."

Johnny shook his head. "Do you really think our folks are going to believe that we went with you willingly?"

"Maybe not, but who knows? I'm not giving up on you guys yet. Dany is ours. Maggie and Bennie . . . well, they're not your average type all-around winners. I don't think either of them won any popularity contests in the old world. As for you, Johnny boy, well, I may have to send you to the happy hunting ground after all. But if you make me do that, put this in your pipe and smoke it—your blond chick belongs to us then."

"A threat like that doesn't do you proud, man," Johnny told him.

"Maybe not, but I'm building a new world, a world for losers. All the losers are going to be winners and all the winners are going to be losers. Dig on that awhile, Geronimo. I'm turning the rotten world upside down." He smiled a little. "But if I ever do have to kill you, Johnny boy, it will be with regret." He closed the engine of the van and gave orders to roll.

It was Suzanne who spotted the jeep as the three stumbled through the darkness of the canyon. She noticed the amber light glowing on the vehicle and she remembered it from Sulphur Springs. "Look, the police!"

"Maybe it's just another trick," Charlie cautioned.

"No, it's really the cops," Red cried, beginning to run toward the jeep. "Hey, Sheriff Rotham! Over here!"

Sheriff Rothman braked the jeep, then turned toward the kids' voices. His flashlight drenched the trio with light. "You kids okay?"

"Yes," Suzanne cried with relief. "Oh, are we *ever* glad to see you!"

"Climb in," the sheriff told them. Getting on his radio, he said, "We picked up three kids." He turned and got their names, relaying the information to the command station in Cinder Creek.

"Is it over, Sheriff?" Suzanne asked eagerly. "Have you captured those maniacs?"

"No, miss," the sheriff said.

"Are our folks okay?" Red asked.

"The people who were locked in the forestry building broke out and called me from Sulphur Springs— sent a messenger for me. Nobody was seriously injured. Police are coming in from all over now, and they've started house-to-house searches. Found some kids locked in the basement of an old stone house and they seemed okay, considering."

Rothman was the sheriff of Sulphur Springs, but he also served the needs of the small surrounding communities should anything important happen. His services hadn't been required in Cinder Creek in a year and a half, and then it had only been a burglary perpetrated by kids.

"Sheriff," Red said heavily, "they killed a girl. . . ."

Rothman turned sharply. "Who?"

"Janet . . . Janet Quantrain."

Rothman relaxed visibly. "No, some mistake there. She was at the forestry building. Sprained leg, but nothing worse. It seems like those guys found her in a ditch in one of the canyons, and they fired their rifles over her head to try to scare her into telling them where her friends were hiding." He paused. "You kids must have been. . . . Anyway, the girl was so hysterical they gave up and took her back into town. Dumped her at the forestry building."

"You see, Red." Suzanne smiled. "All our worries were for nothing. Sheriff, where is Janet now?"

"Her dad took her home."

Suzanne added, "I really should stop at her house to see how she is. Could you stop there for just a moment, Sheriff, and let me run in? She's my closest friend."

"I guess that'd be all right. It's on our way."

The sheriff's jeep stopped at the Quantrain house and Suzanne ran to the door. Janet's parents let Suzanne in, and she hurried directly to the bedroom where Janet lay. "Oh Jan, I'm so happy to see you! We were just sick with worry!"

Janet turned her head on the pillow and looked at Suzanne. "Did Sheriff Rothman find you?"

"Yes. Oh, aren't you glad now we chose to do what we did, Janet? We're safe now. Sheriff Rothman told me a moment ago that those maniacs have just vanished with Johnny and Val and Maggie and Bennie as hostages. God only knows what will happen to them. Aren't you glad we were sensible enough not to turn ourselves over to them when they demanded it?"

A strange smile touched the pale girl's face. "You know something, Suzy? No, I'm not glad. I wish I'd stayed with the others. Because then I'd never have known how selfish I am. And I'd never have known I really didn't have a single friend in the world. Not even . . . not even . . ." She began to cry. "Not even you, Suzy!"

"Why Jan, you're acting stupid. Just because we left you for a minute to take cover? We had to. Did you want us to stay with you and perhaps be shot by those maniacs?"

"Go away, Suzy." Janet turned her head and looked at the wall. "Just, please, go away."

Suzanne turned and ran from the room and then from the house. She climbed quickly into the jeep and it started off.

"How is she?" Red asked.

"Stupid as usual," Suzanne snapped back.

Red was silent a moment. Then he said, "She knows we left her, and she's hurt, isn't she?"

"Oh, so what!" Suzanne said with a toss of her dark hair.

When the jeep arrived in town, there were lawyers, newspapermen—even the FBI had been called into the case as a result of the kidnapping. But those who surged most eagerly toward the jeep were Suzanne's grandparents, Red's father and Charlie's parents. Everyone was crying—eventually even Charlie and his father and Red and his father. Only Suzanne didn't cry. She stared at her grandparents, then said tautly, her chin unsteady, "Please, let's just go home."

The campers traveled in the darkness to a small mesa where the vehicles could be parked among heavy boulders and totally screened from view in all directions. "You know this country pretty good," Johnny told Alex.

He shrugged. "I was born on the Mexican border. My parents were migrant workers. Been all over the Southwest, picking berries, grapes, lettuce, the whole bit. Poor white trash, you know."

"Your folks still live around here?" Johnny was hoping to get close enough to one of them to get an ally. He didn't have any hope with Attila, and Garibaldi was too slow to be of any help. Eric was vicious, and a plea to him would probably have netted a broken skull.

Alex laughed softly. "No. My daddy lives at San Quentin and my mama went to wherever cheating ladies go when they stop breathing. You see, my daddy had just one good thing in his whole miserable life going for him—he had a pretty lady. I remember seeing Mama in her cheap clothes and thinking she had a face twice as good as most of those movie ladies. She was Daddy's one good thing and then one night he came home and he found out he didn't even have that one good thing. He shot them both."

"Must have been rough for you," Johnny said.

"At first, but I made out all right. I found all kinds of friends to help me through—red and blue and yellow, all sitting in a bottle."

Attila gathered the four hostages. "I'm going to be real gentlemanly about this. The guys will sleep with one wrist handcuffed to a camper wheel, but the girls will be free to fly if they feel like it. The only drawback to that is, if we find the chicks gone, the guys get shot." He threw down a sleeping bag at the front wheel of each camper and tossed sleeping bags to the girls. Then he handcuffed Johnny and Bennie to the wheels.

The moon bobbed into view, flooding the mesa, but since the campers were parked between boulders in the narrow gorge, the night illumination wouldn't be of much help to the searchers.

Attila allowed no fires. He furnished the same kind of cold sandwiches for the hostages that he and his companions had. From time to time planes roared overhead and Johnny figured they must be searching for them, but how could they see anything?

Theodora came over to Johnny and knelt beside him for a moment. "Probably tomorrow we'll be over the border. Attila knows a good place we can hide down there. Johnny . . ." Her eyes clouded. "Attila won't wait forever for you to make up your mind. I mean . . . won't you please join us?"

"Dora, listen. This whole business is crazy. If you help us get away, I promise to help you later on."

Her eyes turned cold. "I was in the water. San Francisco Bay. It was the second time I'd tried . . . and he was there, pulling me out. Attila, I mean. He doesn't love me or anything like that but he's been good to me. Real good. Johnny, if you don't join us, then Attila will kill you. He told me that."

Johnny closed his eyes. He heard her breathing hard. "Listen, Johnny, being one of us is better than dying. I mean, I was almost dead and I know. Please Johnny." She waited another moment, then she walked away.

12. "But We Had Some Good Ideas"

In the morning, before the sun had even appeared, Attila and his companions woke up their hostages. The boys were briefly released from their handcuffs, and everybody had a quick, cold breakfast. Johnny watched Attila climb to the highest point of the mesa to scan the countryside for possible pursuers. Johnny followed him, hoping to make another try at talking him into freeing his hostages. In spite of what Theodora had said, Johnny couldn't believe Attila would murder anybody.

Attila searched the vast surrounding wilderness through field glasses. When, abruptly, a strap on the glasses broke, he made a quick move to retrieve them. That movement brought him too close to the edge. The rocks beneath his feet gave way, and he slid over the edge of the mesa.

Only Johnny was close enough to see what had happened. He ran to the spot and looked over, seeing that Attila had broken his fall by grabbing a scrub oak. He hung by just that, with about a hundred-foot drop beneath his dangling feet. If he lost his grip, as he soon would, he would be dashed to death within seconds in the bed of the shallow creek below. A sardonic smile touched his pale lips as he recognized the face that came over the edge. "You got the last laugh after all, eh, Geronimo?" He was losing his grip so rapidly that even if he yelled for help, his friends could never reach him in time.

Johnny dropped to his stomach and ripped off his leather belt. He wrapped one end tightly around his wrist and hand and dropped the other end to Attila. "Grab onto this. Slowly—that oak is slipping."

Attila transferred his grip gingerly from the scrub oak to the belt, just minutes before the shrub uprooted and went tumbling down the slope. Johnny screamed for help, bringing Garibaldi and Alex on the run. They saw the situation and Alex grabbed rope from one of the vans. Within a few minutes they had Attila pulled to safety.

In the momentary confusion, Johnny saw a chance to escape. There was no one back at the campers but Eric. If Johnny could get there first, surprise Eric and grab his rifle, perhaps he could get the others loaded in a van and get away. It was a slim chance, but a chance.

As Johnny turned and started quickly down to the vans, a voice crackled behind him. "Hold it, Geronimo." It was Attila's, and he held a pistol at Johnny's back.

Johnny turned wearily. Attila looked straight at him. "Why, Johnny boy? Why didn't you just let me drop and improve the odds?"

"Chalk up one for the squares," Johnny said wryly. "Or for the fools!"

"Like I said," Attila spoke slowly, "if I ever have to kill you, man, it will be with regrets."

Sheriff Mike Rothman gathered in the civic building with Charles Harrison, Jim Roman and Bennie's and Margaret's parents. Rothman was a big, beefy man, direct in manner. "From this note, gentlemen, we are led to believe that your kids went willingly with these characters. I don't know your kids. I have no idea what kinds of problems you've been having with them. I'd like you all to be frank with me because it will make my job that much easier."

Charles Harrison was tall and dark, a handsome man who looked many years younger than his actual age at ordinary times, but in these past days he'd aged visibly. "Johnny is the most dependable kid in the world. There's not a doubt in my mind that he was forced to sign their proclamation."

Jim Roman was a slight, wiry man with thinning hair, blond. "Valerie's a good girl. She's always been as honest with us as we've been with her. They must have made her sign it."

"How about your girl?" Rothman asked Margaret's father.

"Never," he said. "Maggie is tough and independent."

Bennie's father nodded agreement. "Bennie wouldn't take off like that—not my son."

"All right. From what the other kids say, these characters are on something. Drugs, probably. They're likely to be dangerous and the longer they have the hostages, the more chance there is of something happening. The teachers told me they were really rough when they took over the school. Mr. Farnsworth said one of them was crazy for sure."

Suzanne had been asked by the sheriff to answer a few additional questions, and she came into the civic building with her grandparents. "What did they seem like to you?" Rothman asked the girl.

"I only saw them from a distance. They carried rifles and they had weird medallions around their necks. I've read about people like them in the papers and magazines—weird types, interested in the occult. I wouldn't be surprised if they were totally insane the way they looked."

Jim Roman winced at the description, thinking of his girl out there somewhere with people like that. Mr. Illiam shared an agonized look with Roman.

Suzanne noticed the apprehensive looks on the older men's faces. "I'm sorry. I really tried to convince Maggie and Val to come with us into the mountains when those maniacs told us to surrender to them. It just didn't make any sense to go like a fly into a spider's web, but the girls wouldn't see it sensibly. I'm sure I don't know whatever possessed them to do something so foolish."

"I understand. They feared for their families and for Johnny," Jim Roman said softly. "I was talking to Hugh and Sandy and they said the threat was pretty explicit that people would get shot if they didn't cooperate."

"But still," Suzanne said, "wouldn't you have preferred for Val not to be so noble, Mr. Roman?"

"Yes," Jim Roman said emphatically. "God help me, yes! But she isn't like that. She never was and I guess she never could be."

"Well," Sheriff Rothman said, breaking the awkward pause, "we're going to do the best we can."

The two-van caravan stopped at midmorning. Alex knew every nook and cranny of the wilderness. "I was a lonely kid," he explained. "And this is the place my folks stayed the longest. I spent most of my time hiking around. It was better than sitting home watching Mama making a fool out of Daddy. I guess I got a pretty good map of the territory in my brain."

Bennie was alone a few minutes with Margaret and he whispered, "Last night I'm sure I heard search planes."

Margaret had washed her hair in the creek and she was now starting to rebraid it. "I heard them too."

"Maggie, don't put it in a braid," Bennie said.

"What?" She stared at him in amazement.

"I mean, it's such a bother, isn't it?" Bennie flushed, his neck crimsoning first, then his entire face.

"I happen to think it's the most comfortable way to keep it." Margaret continued to stare at the boy. "Bennie, what on earth is the matter with you?"

"Oh, nothing I guess. It just looked so pretty and coppery hanging free . . . but never mind." He cleared his throat. "If there is a search on, I think we better figure out what to do when they close in."

Maggie nodded, her long brown hair in wavy profusion around her small face, the braid remaining undone. "They'll go berserk and shoot us all if they think they're trapped."

"The way I figure, if we see the police, we've got to jump them any way we can, Johnny and I."

"Johnny and you? Why not all of us? I can scratch and kick and bite like you wouldn't believe, Bennie Bryce," Margaret declared, almost gleefully. Bennie

131

suppressed a smile. "Aw, Maggie, you're a girl, five feet tall, eighty pounds at the outside."

Margaret lifted her chin defiantly. "My vital statistics have nothing to do with it. Nor my sex. Women have long been known to be fiercer than men. Haven't you ever read about the female of the species in the animal kingdom? What do you think a she-bear does if her cubs are threatened—whimpers for her mate? You better believe it, she doesn't. Bennie, the so-called weakness of women is a myth cultivated by egotistical males."

"Okay Maggie—we'll all jump them. I'll get the word to Johnny and Val, so we're all agreed on a single plan."

Bennie reached Johnny and passed the word along. If the police showed up, they would try to overwhelm their captors by surprise.

Margaret observed Attila standing by himself, and she developed a sudden plan of her own. Perhaps Bennie's silly little comment about her hair had inspired it. Attila kept a pistol always stuck in his belt, and Margaret figured that if she could distract him, she might get it and capture him. Without Attila's leadership, Margaret felt, the others might crumble.

Margaret fluffed her hair around her face and moved toward Attila. She despised coy female tricks on ordinary occasions but this was an emergency. When Attila saw her, he crushed out his cigarette. "Is that where you get your courage?" she asked him, recognizing the scent of grass.

"I get my cool where I can find it," he answered back. "I imagine your old man has his little drugs."

"No. He disapproves of crutches of that kind."

"Whoopee. What about nicotine? Or happy hour? Or maybe sleeping pills at beddy-bye time?"

"My father always says that all a man needs is a clear conscience and then he should have no trouble functioning."

Attila looked more closely at the girl. "Tell me, did you let your hair down for me, little girl?"

Margaret shrugged and looked away. She wasn't very good at this sort of thing. "Well, you're actually rather nice-looking, Attila."

He smiled oddly. "I never had you figured for this, Maggie. I saw you as one of those bright types, cool, tough, who don't dig guys all that much."

"You're not right about everything," Margaret said, forcing her protesting lips into a smile and flashing her eyes. She was certain that if she could only get close enough, she could grab the pistol and aim it at him. He was the brains of the group, the most dangerous.

Attila's smile continued. "Want a kiss, Maggie?"

She came to him—but then, when she was a foot away, he reached out and grabbed her wrists, a triumphant sneer on his lips. "Honey, you'd rather kick my teeth in than kiss me. Who do you think you're fooling? You just want to get close enough to get those conniving little female hands on my gun. And then, I do believe, you'd have the guts to shoot me."

He continued to hold her wrists in a tight grip. "You really take me for pretty stupid, little girl. Now you listen—you go tell your friends that any tricks, any fancy little schemes, and you've all had it. This is war, honey—no quarter given. If you've read your history books, then you know how good old Napoleon sacrificed hundred of thousands of Frenchmen when he marched across Russia—for what? For his dream of glory. So maybe we got to sacrifice a few of you. Get it?" With that he shoved her away.

Margaret returned to the others, disconsolate. "I blew it," she groaned to Bennie. "I tried to sweet-talk that creep Attila and he saw right through me."

Bennie looked at her sympathetically. "Anyway, you tried."

"Oh, but it wasn't good enough! It was worse than not trying at all," Margaret scolded herself.

Valerie stood a few yards off staring across the small meadow, her eyes on Johnny. She wondered whether next week this would all be a bad memory? Whether, in June, she would be going to the prom with Johnny? Whether she would ever see her parents again.

It was late afternoon when a plume of smoke stained the horizon. Bennie had been looking out the back window of the second van and he stiffened, his heart pounding. He squinted his eyes and tried to identify the oncoming vehicle, wondering whether it could perhaps be the police. In the next moment Eric too spotted the vehicle in his rear-view mirror. "Hey! Somebody's coming!"

Alex turned around and looked. "Seems like an old pickup truck."

"Probably some kids looking for Mexico," Bennie suggested, trying to calm their apprehension.

"Well, they're gonna find trouble if they come near us," Eric said menacingly.

Alex held his rifle in readiness and spoke to the next van. "Hey, Attila, there's a pickup coming up behind us."

"Keep cool," Attila said. "Very cool."

The pickup truck came nearer. There was canvas over the bed in back and a few flakes of hay piled on the canvas.

"Maybe just farmers or brush-rabbit hunters," Bennie said. Eric looked harder. "Appears to be a couple of old farmers."

"Maybe some of their cattle ranged too far south and they're looking for calves. Ranchers do that sometimes." Perspiration streamed over Bennie's manacled wrists. He recognized Sheriff Rothman driving the truck and his deputy beside him.

"They got hay in the back of the truck all right," Eric said.

"Coming closer now," Alex advised the lead van.

"Don't do anything," Attila instructed. "If they stop, see what they want before you start the fireworks. Could be just stupid old local types."

As the pickup truck came alongside, Sheriff Rothman leaned out the window. He wore a battered straw hat and denim bib overalls. "Howdee thar," he drawled out the side window. "Y'all know the way to Tinker's Well?"

Alex answered out the side, "No, never heard of it, friend. Sorry."

"Thet so?" Rothman played his part well, chewing his tobacco diligently. "I'm pert near outta water in my radiator. Figured to fill 'er up at Tinker's. You boys wouldn't have none t'spare, wouldja?"

Alex shook his head. "No, man. Sorry."

Dany, who had been asleep between Alex and Eric, woke up and stared through the window at the man in the pickup. "Oh. Hi, Sheriff Rothman," she said sleepily. He had brought her home once when she ran away to Sulphur Springs.

"Cops!" Alex screamed at the lead van. Instantly, four armed men jumped from under the canvas in the back of the pickup, and in the same moment, Bennie and Margaret leaped at the two men in their van. Margaret clawed violently and Bennie kicked while the police yanked open the doors, dragging a stunned Alex and Eric out. Dora, no fight in her at all, followed docilely. In the front van, Johnny and Valerie tried to do the same as Margaret and Bennie had accomplished, but the element of surprise was gone. Garibaldi drove Johnny back with the rifle and the lead van roared ahead at full speed with Sheriff Rothman and his young sandy-haired deputy in pursuit.

Attila turned sharply into the canyon, then saw it was a dead end. "Give up," Johnny pleaded with him. "You got no way out."

Garibaldi's eyes burned dully. "You want I should finish them, Attila?"

Attila glanced back, his eyes fusing for a moment with Johnny's. There was a wildness in those dark eyes, the terrible look of something doomed. He braked the van and jumped out, grabbing Valerie's wrist and dragging her forward up a narrow canyon trail. Garibaldi jabbed the rifle butt into Johnny's spine, driving him ahead. They stopped at a rocky vantage point and both Attila and Garibaldi aimed their rifles down at the approaching pickup truck. Rothman had a bullhorn, and from behind the stopped truck, he shouted, "Come on down you guys—hands up. You're trapped."

Johnny knew that the place would be a battleground of gunfire in a moment. He looked at Valerie, something turning inside him. "Please, man, let my girl go."

Attila's face carried a strange smile at the request.

He shrugged and said to Valerie, "Go on down." Then he looked at Johnny. "Chalk up one for the weirdos, or for the fools. . . ."

"I'm not going without you, Johnny," Valerie cried, but Johnny answered her harshly. "Go—go *now*." And Johnny yelled to Sheriff Rothman, "Don't fire—a girl is coming down!" Valerie stumbled down the trail, tears blinding her eyes.

Attila knelt behind a boulder and fired at Sheriff Rothman once the girl was clear. A fierce volley of gunfire came in reply. Garibaldi let out an agonized cry when Attila fell. He dropped to his own knees, as if struck himself, suddenly a scarecrow deprived of its stick skeleton. He cried like a child, collapsing into himself.

The sheriff knew it was all over, and he came running with his deputy. He looked at Johnny who knelt beside Attila. "You okay?" Johnny nodded. "Get help for him. He's shot. . . ."

Attila's face was turning pale, but he managed one more grin. "We had some good ideas, Geronimo. Maybe we were crazy, but we had some good ideas, didn't we, man?"

"Yeah," Johnny whispered. "Sure, man."